ENEMIES BE FRIENDS

The Beginning

Written And Illustrated By: E. A. Andersen

Order this book online at www.trafford.com
or email orders@trafford.com

Most Trafford titles are also available at major online book retailers.

Printed in the United States of America.

ISBN: 978-1-4269-4254-9 (sc)

Trafford rev. 07/09/2011

 www.trafford.com

North America & international
toll-free: 1 888 232 4444 (USA & Canada)
phone: 250 383 6864 ♦ fax: 812 355 4082

CONTENTS

INTRODUCTION

Several years ago there lived two races of aliens on a planet far in our solar system called Lempton, but its existence didn't last long. The two races were called Lemptions and Vieniems. Lemptions were peaceful creatures that existed in beautiful valleys and grew crystals from beautiful flowers living in the east of Planet Lempton. While the Vieniems, who were evil and hateful aliens, perched on mountains and in caves in the west of the planet. One day their planet was destroyed, so they began to fight with each other thinking the other was responsible for their planet's destruction. So the only place of refuge for the last existing Lemptions and Vieniems was on a planet called Earth, the closes life bearing planet to Lempton. So they existed on the planet Earth on different sides for years, but the rivalry still lives on, while Vieniems kill hundreds of Lemptions off every year. Now the Lemptions are hiding in secret behind the lives of humans, despised of their differences. They await the day a hero will emerge to bring peace between the two races. Still on going, Vieniems hiding secretly still go on killing Lemptions attempting to destroy and end their race forever...

After a long wait a hero arrives.

Chapter 1

Things Turn

"Aliza, WAKE UP! You have to make breakfast," called Aliza's Step- Mom, Hanna, who was pounding on the door of the attic.

Aliza was now nineteen years of age and was very beautiful and had white fair skin. Aliza got up and brushed her white hair and itched her white furry ears. Then she put on a black hat to cover her ears because they weren't human, but cat-like sticking out from the right and left corners of her head. Finally, she dressed herself in her old raggedy school uniform with tears in the skirt and then she slipped on torn stockings. However, she found that her step-grandma's old shoes practically squeezed her feet after she pounded them on with extreme difficulty.

Once she got out of the attic and went down a small staircase, she continued off to the kitchen.

"Come on, Aliza! I'M STARVING!" said her brother, Ryan, with his butt cheeks literally hanging off the side's of the kitchen stool.

"Yeah, young lady. Next time you sleep in, you can forget …that dress from your step grandmother," said Luke, Aliza's So-Called-Step-Father.

"Yeah, an old moth eaten hand-me-down," thought Aliza in disgust.

"Yeah...well maybe if I hadn't had so many chores," said Aliza, while she tried to sound innocent.

"Don't you start!" said Luke with an evil look, as he warned her not to go any further.

Aliza finished making the food and gave everyone a plate with a four stack of pancakes and herself one because she knew the consequences of taking more.

"Well...you have to start school." said Luke.

"Yeah, that's right. And Aliza you'd better not skip anymore school. And start another year over again." said Hanna viciously to Aliza.

"Yeah, but like I told you. WE CAN'T WEAR HATS IN SCHOOL!" said Aliza, as she gestured to the hat she had on.

"ENOUGH...as I said before. YOU COULD tape your ears down and cover them with your hair." said Hanna, as if she was trying to be patient.

"BUT IT HURTS! And it still won't stop the kids from bothering me about my hair color or clothes." said Aliza, as she tried to be reasonable.

"OH WELL!" said Luke, who was smirking evilly.

"Now both of you go to your bus stop," said Hanna.

As Hanna spoke, she gave Ryan a nice lunch box and Aliza an old paper lunch bag, which was a little damp at the bottom.

Ryan left out the door pleased, as Aliza followed gloomily.

While they were halfway down the block, Ryan almost immediately ripped off Aliza's hat.

"Hey, GIVE THAT BACK!!!" yelled Aliza startled.

Aliza jumped for it from his hand but it was out of her reach because he was to tall.

"Even if you wear this...YOUR STILL going to look like a freak?" said Ryan teasing.

Aliza's eyes started to glow purple.

"Give it BACK YOU JERK!" said Aliza angered.

At that moment, Ryan threw Aliza's hat into a nearby open sewer.

Aliza gasped.

She slowly walked up to the edge of the man hole and stared into the dark sewer in horror.

Then Aliza looked up to Ryan.

"Get It Back!" yelled Aliza angered.

"TOO LATE!" said Ryan with a crude smile, as he pointed to their bus that was driving up the street.

"Oh man," thought Aliza, as she tried to fold her ears down.

The bus stopped and opened the doors.

Ryan went on the bus, as Aliza followed with an exasperated sigh.

Then Aliza saw the bus driver stare, while the kids laughed and pointed at her clothes and head.

Ryan sat all the way at the front of the bus next to his girlfriend, as Aliza slid to the back of the bus.

She sat and placed her bag next to her, but as she did… she saw that she was sitting next to another person.

When Aliza looked up she was stunned.

Even though, that person was facing the bus window, she saw the exact same features she had only red hair and red furry ears.

Then suddenly something popped in her head.

"Zack?" asked Aliza slowly.

He turned around.

"OH MY GOSH…" he said.

Smiles were suddenly slapped on both of their faces.

"ZACK, I CAN'T BELIEVE THIS. LAST TIME I SAW YOU … were…was …IT'S BEEN SO LONG!" said Aliza, as she jumped up in excitement.

"GOSH! I Missed SOOOO much!" said Zack, as he got up to give her a hug.

"I missed you, too," said Aliza.

"HEY FREAKS...Why don't you sit down...WHILE I'M DRIVING!" yelled the bus driver angrily.

Zack and Aliza both sat down quickly.

"I Have So Much To Tell You!" said Aliza.

"Oh, let me go first!" exclaimed Zack quickly.

"OKAaaaaaaY!" said Aliza in a goofy voice.

They both laughed joyfully...finally being reunited, after their long lasting separation.

"We're supposed to be brought to the school today...my parents recently told me," said Zack.

"What do you mean?" asked Aliza with a confused look.

"You don't know?" asked Zack with a goofy smile.

Aliza looked confused and shook her head.

"Oh my, ooookay...let me start from the beginning. We...our kind...come from the Planet Lempton. When our planet was destroyed decades ago...we had to settle on this earth and coincide and live with humans. At a certain point in age we are able to transform. So the school is to teach us and learn about our kind," whispered Zack.

Aliza's mouth just hung open stunned by what she just heard.

"Are you okay?" asked Zack.

Then she bursted out laughing.

"Okay you're weird!" said Zack, as he looked away.

"No, no, no...it's just that I've always wondered why...I was different. I mean...I've always lived with actual humans and since I last saw you...I've always thought there was no ONE like you and me. AND NOW THE...the blanks are filled in," said Aliza with a smile and was laughing on the inside.

"Really, YOU never knew? It's just a simple answer," said Zack a little shocked.

"No…and what's a Lemption, how do we transform? I know we are Lemps now… but Lemptions?" asked Aliza in excitement.

"Well…my parents showed me, how they transform. They use these stones that were given to them from the school…grown from grains provided, saved, and reproduced from Planet Lempton…saved by generations. They encourage us to transform into a cat-like werewolf," explained Zack.

"Anything Special?" asked Aliza.

"Well, nothing really. We're just bigger than before, we are very strong, great jumping abilities, we heal faster then normal humans, and our howls are extremely loud, being heard from miles away and have something special and different happen for each individual Lemption's howl," said Zack.

"What do we have them for, I mean…why were they given to us?" asked Aliza.

"Well…we used them to defend ourselves against Veniems…that were on the other side of our Planet…And unfortunately it's the same here?" said Zack.

"Wait! What do you mean 'unfortunately it's the same here'? What are Veniems…ARE we in danger of them?" said Aliza quickly.

"Gees…you ask a lot!" said Zack.

"Well…I told you WHY. Please, answer the question… I'm curious," said Aliza desperately.

"Okay…their ears are pointed, with their human form… otherwise all look human when transformed…without a stone by the way. Not to mention…ummm…to kill us they must bite five seconds worth to inject venom. And they also have wings to fly and we don't. And they can also transform into us, which is really dangerous for you and I," said Zack gloomily.

"How can they transform into us!?" excliamed Aliza almost immediately.

"Well...There were myths that once Veneims and Lemptions lived together peacefully on our Planet...and sickens me to say this...married and had kids together...so few of the Vieniems that exist today can transform into one of us because of some of our blood that still runs in their veins...but only once in their entire lifetime can they ever transform into a Lemption...and only for a short period of time," explained Zack.

Zack saw Aliza's expression of unbelieving disgust and tears of fear.

Zack quickly responded.

"No worries though…as far as I know WE ARE SAFE as long as we stay on our side of the region," explained Zack surely.

"Wow!" said Aliza still with an unbelieving expression, as she shook her head.

At that moment…the bus stopped, and everyone started to exist.

Aliza and Zack were the last to exist.

Since, they were still quite early they headed towards a nearby bench and sat side by side.

"Now …just so you know, we have to be picked up…no where near here or other humans," said Zack.

"That will be hard," said Aliza optimistically.

"Why?" asked Zack with a weird look.

"Well...Maybe not...because of HIM!" said Aliza.

She pointed.

Zack turned and saw an oversized boy kissing a girl.

"THAT'S THE LITTLE BABY... I SAW A LONG TIME AGO IN YOUR STEP MOM'S ARMS!" said Zack quietly with a smile.

"Yep...not so little anymore," whispered Aliza in reply.

"Noooo kidding...and they call us freaks," said Zack under his breath.

They both looked at each other and bursted in loud hysterical laughs.

"Alright let's go," said Zack grabbing Aliza's hand suddenly.

"Come on...wait a minute ...YOU...Aaare...nineteen years old, right?" asked Zack with a quick thought.

"Yes," said Aliza raising an eyebrow.

"THEN COME ON!" said Zack starting off towards a nearby forest.

Aliza followed behind.

"Why this way?" asked Aliza.

"To avoid being seen... by humans," said Zack.

Zack shook his head with a smile at the thought of Aliza's cluelessness of her heritage.

"Oh," said Aliza, as she thought about everything she just learned in the past ten minutes.

So they continued through the forest.

Chapter 2

Surprise, Surprise

"So when do you think they'll get here?" asked Aliza.

"Soon...I'm sure," said Zack.

"How do they know where to find us?" asked Aliza.

"My parents told me that they'd pick me up here so..." said Zack and finished his response with a shrug of his shoulders.

They were sitting alone on large stones in a field surrounded by trees.

"You know...even though, we haven't known each other for a long time. When I was looking at your step brother...a thought crossed my mind," said Zack.

"Really...What?" asked Aliza looking curious.

"Well, you see... ummm...when we go to the school we'll be chosen one by one to be mates for life, husband and wife, by the school and...I figured if we say we're already a couple. Then we wouldn't have to worry about getting stuck with someone we wouldn't like or know," said Zack.

"What...Why!?" exclaimed Aliza dumbfounded.

"They do that because our kind is...well...not very populated," said Zack.

"That's not fair. How...Why?" asked Aliza in angry tears.

Aliza stood on her feet in rage.

"How are we 'not very populated'?" asked Aliza.

"Because of Vieniem attacks?" explained Zack gloomily.

"Sooo..." continued Zack waiting for a response.

Aliza looked at him with a teary frown and slowly sat back down.

"I know it's been a long time...and this is so sudden ...But I want you to know that, I think you're a beautiful Lemption and I'll always care about you," explained Zack.

"Really?" said Aliza as a smile crossed her lips.

"Yes," said Zack.

Aliza rested her head on his shoulder.

"Could this be the start of a better life?" thought Aliza closing her eyes.

Suddenly, there was the sound of rattling reins and horses.

"They're here," said Zack.

Aliza opened her eyes to behold a huge blue carriage being pulled by a dozen white horses.

"The coach is beautiful," thought Aliza.

The door opened and a Lemption maid walked out.

"Welcome," said the maid with black hair and black furry ears.

When Zack and Aliza boarded the coach, they found that the interior was beautiful and luxurious.

"Here we go," said the maid.

She handed both Zack and Aliza a set of clothes and shoes.

"Thank you," said Aliza surprised.

"Restrooms are right there," said the maid pointing to doors at the back.

After Aliza changed, she looked at herself in the mirror stunned.

The dress had gold suns and moons on it made of navy silk that reached her feet. Then the high heel shoes were made of navy satin and had gemmed buckles.

When she walked out the door, she found Zack in a well dressed black suit and black bow tie.

Zack looked at her with soft eyes.

"You look beautiful," said Zack with a warm flutter in his stomach.

Aliza blushed.

Zack and Aliza sat down on two black leather chairs to wait for their arrival to the school.

Chapter 3

The Ceremony

Aliza and Zack were on the coach till evening. They were eating a crumb cake, as the coach came to a halt.

Some of the other students looked out the windows.

"We've arrived!" called the maid after she came from behind a curtain.

Zack and Aliza stood up to brush off the crumbs and joined the group of students outside.

Aliza noticed more coaches unloading and the many different colors, shapes, and sizes of Lemptions like her unboarding.

She was about to cry.

However, she noticed that two different cat-like ear shapes depicted the woman lemptions from the males because all the womans ears extended out longer and with more feathery soft fur.

She grabbed Zack's hand, so they wouldn't get lost in the crowd.

"This way to the Ceremony!" called a Lemption servant with brown hair and white furry ears.

"Ceremony?' asked Aliza a little confused.

"Yeah, that's where they announce couples, cottages and crystals. My parents explained it to me," said Zack.

As they walked, Aliza saw beautiful cottages and stone walkways. There were square gardens in between blocks of cottages.

"Its beautiful," said Aliza stunned.

"I know," nodded Zack in agreement.

They came to a large arch stone entryway with a big wooden door.

When they went through they came to a huge castle and as they entered the main hallway of the castle, there were marble floors with stone walls inside.

"The ceremony is in the dining room!" called another Lemption maid with silver hair and pink furry ears.

When they went in Zack and Aliza saw circular tables with white table cloths and beautiful crystal wear. There was also a vase with a rose and two chairs at each table in the huge ballroom.

Other older Lemption students were already seated at the tables.

When Aliza looked at the front stage there was an old Lemption with a gray beard and black ears waiting and behind him were more Lemption teachers sitting at a large table.

"Welcome to Lempschool. I am Principal Hartford," he echoed.

The principle looked at the group of students with a smile.

"First, rules of the school are to be followed at all times or detention. No one is to transform outside of school grounds and yes...cottages and garden court yards are part of school grounds. If anyone has cubs, there is a new preschool daycare found with Miss Perch in the fifth hallway during school hours," echoed Principal Hartford.

A short stout teacher stood up and waved her hand.

"Kids...yeah right," said Aliza.

Zack laughed.

"But why do they call them cubs, hmmm? Could it be because of what we transform into. Cat-like werewolf? That's what Zack told me." thought Aliza.

"Unfortunately, NOBODY is to be outside their cottages after dark!" echoed Principle Hartford again.

Aliza was startled because her thinking was interrupted.

"Why?" said a student in the crowd.

To this the principle stared down the group with a serious face.

"Because of the recent Vieniem attacks," responded Hartford.

Zack and Aliza looked at each other with fear.

The principal continued.

"I will call everyone up by name and you will be presented with your crystal, key to a cottage, and a marriage mate. You are officially married after you are paired, but a wedding is not necessary. Your mate will be chosen. If you already have someone in mind please say after your crystal is presented to you...you will be given only one right to choose a mate for life if you wish," said the principal.

The principal was handed a large book by another teacher and opened it.

"Zack Guideheart!" declared the principal.

"That's me," said Zack.

Aliza watched him go up on the stage and saw the principal hand him a gold box and a key with the number fourteen on it.

Zack opened the gold box with a smile and slid on a gold chain with a red crystal attached.

"Transform," said the Principal.

Suddenly, Zack's form completely changed before Aliza's eyes.

Aliza's mouth hung open in amazement.

Zack was four times larger with fur all over him, added with a tail. His face was cat-like and his hands and feet had huge black claws. Instead, of a werewolf he was a were cat.

All new comers awed in amazement.

"Nice," thought Aliza.

"Now...do you already have a person you wish to have as a marriage mate? You only have one choice choose wisely," asked the Principle.

"Yes," said Zack.

"Then please introduce her," said the principle.

Zack gestured to Aliza to come up on the stage.

Then Aliza blushed and came up on the stage.

Once she walked next to Zack everything became quite and everyone stared at Aliza.

Aliza looked at Zack confused and he just shrugged his shoulders.

"Is it her?" asked a teacher nearest to the Principle.

"I...it...it is," he said.

"Isn't she the chosen one?" called a student.

"Chosen who?" chuckled Aliza.

"No way!" exclaimed Zack.

"She's the chosen one! It's Aliza Rain!" echoed the Principle with a huge smile.

"What do you mean?" said Aliza frantically.

"You're the one to help us defeat the Vieniems for good, so we no longer have to live in threat of them," said the teacher excitedly.

"How do you know?" said Aliza.

Aliza's heart was pounding in her ears.

"You're hair and ears are as pure white as the Pearl color of Pleets Mountain Snow...and your eyes are as the mountain's purple crystal base. The Chosen Ones Features!" explained the principal.

"Did you know?" asked Aliza looking intensely at Zack.

"I've only heard stories from my parents, but I never would have guessed," said Zack honestly.

"So I have a crystal, too?" asked Aliza.

"You're blessed with the gift of transforming without a crystal. As well as special powers and unique transformation," said the principal.

"What transformation and powers?" asked Aliza.

"They're unknown...even to us," said the Principal.

Aliza was stunned by everything that was just said to her and began to feel overwhelmed.

"But I haven't transformed ever in my life!" bursted Aliza.

"You'll bloom as soon as you're ready," said the Principal.

"When?" asked Aliza.

"I'm not sure...only you'll know when," said the Principal.

"OH GREAT!" thought Aliza.

"Welcome...The Chosen One!" called out the principal.

Then the entire ballroom yelled out in cheer and applause.

Aliza turned red.

She felt Zack put his arm around her and they walked to a table to eat, as the rest of the newcomers were being presented with a crystal, cottage key, and a marriage mate.

Chapter 4

A Night to Remember

Aliza and Zack were walking down the stone path from the finished ceremony.

"I can't believe you're the chosen one," said Zack, as he strecthed from a full stomach.

"Yeah right," said Aliza, who was rarely able to take a single bite do to all the starring Lemptions that were around their table.

"Oh come on, don't be like that," said Zack.

"Well...think...I have so much responsibility now," said Aliza with a frown on her face.

"Yeah...I know. Not to mention, everyone will want to be your friend now...you're famous. Good thing we were the first ones to be paired," replied Zack.

"I can't wait," said Aliza sarcastically.

"We're here," said Zack suddenly.

There was a beautiful cottage surrounded by flowers with a white gate at the base with with the gold numbers fourteen on the door.

When they walked up to the door Zack took out the key that was handed to him at the ceremony and unlocked it.

When they walked in their cottage they saw a hall with red carpeting and a bathroom that had blue, black, and white tiles on the floors and walls. The kitchen had peach tiles on the floor with wooden oak cabinets with pink counter tops. Then there was also a large refrigerator and a large freezer next to a beautiful brass stove. Then when they reached the end of the hall there was a master bedroom with two dressers.

However, there was only one king size bed.

Aliza and Zack looked at each other and laughed.

"I'm not sleeping on the floor," said Zack, as he looked at Aliza's willful face.

"You have got to be kidding," said Aliza.

Aliza went to the dresser on the left and opened it to find a pretty light-blue lace underwear and half top along with many different others.

She held it up.

"Nice, can't wait to see you in that," said Zack.

"SHUT UP!!!" shouted Aliza angered.

She grabbed the set.

"I sure hope they have pajamas," thought Aliza desparately, as she rummaged through the drawers in a panic.

She found a light blue gown in the next drawer.

"I'm getting dressed," said Aliza in a huff.

"Fine, I'll get dressed out here," said Zack.

Aliza went to get changed in the bathroom.

Aliza came out a few minutes later with the gown to her mid thigh.

"Okay, I'm done," said Aliza.

Zack had on just a pair of red plaid pants with the gold chain a red crystal still around his neck.

Zack turned around from the other side of the bed. His stomach fluttered up in an instant, as he watched her beautiful curved figure make its way to the bed. He watched every step she made intensely and when he saw her mid thigh exposed his adrenaline began to rush with a pulse.

THUD!

Zack fell off the bed.

"You're such a dork," chuckled Aliza, as she slid under the covers.

Suddenly, Zack heard scratching on the door down the hall.

"Wha...what's that?" stuttered Aliza.

"I don't know," said Zack.

The scratching got louder with a banging.

Zack instantly transformed and made his way into the door, as Aliza hid under the covers.

His figure almost reached the ceiling of the cottage.

Zack reached the door handle prepared to leap on who ever dared to come on his territory.

The door opened to reveal that Principal Hartford was shaking in sweat and had a worried face.

Zack detransformed back to his normal self confused.

"The...The...they struck," said the principal struck with fear.

"Who?" said Zack.

"The Vieniems struck and killed one of the newcomers," said the principal.

"But how? Everyone returned to their cottages on time," said Aliza suddenly.

"A girl got mad at her chosen mate and ran into the garden courtyards. I guess they sensed the chosen one and were after you, Aliza," said the principal.

"So that girl died because of me," said Aliza.

Her eyes began to fill with tears.

Zack walked to Aliza and sat next to her on the bed and held her close.

"So why did you come here to tell us?" asked Zack with a frown.

"I...I...I came here to check on you guys, to make sure the chosen one and you were alright," stuttered the principal.

"Yeah, right! You were scared, hoping we could protect you," called Zack furiously.

Aliza began to wail quietly on Zack's shoulder.

"Perhaps I should go," said the principal, as he exited.

"Yeah, thanks for the good news," thought Zack sarcastically.

Zack looked sorrowfully at Aliza, who was still crying profusely.

"Come on, we should get some sleep," said Zack softly.

"I...it's my entire fault. I...if I was...wasn't here. She...She never would have died," choked Aliza, as she covered herself with the fleece blanket.

Zack switched off the light.

Zack got in the bed and put his arm around her to assure her some comfort.

As Zack listened to her cry herself asleep, he felt sorry for her. He realized being The Chosen One isn't what it was cracked up to be.

Then time passed and Aliza and Zack finally drifted to sleep.

Chapter 5

A Nightmare Beginning

Zack awoke to the sunlight shining through the window and noticed Aliza was still asleep.

Zack looked at Aliza's head poking from under the covers. He heard her snoring with a soft quiet purring growl.

"Awe...how cute," thought Zack.

Zack got up and went into the dresser and pulled out a pair of cargo pants and black shirt.

Zack pulled off the pajama pants.

"Nice boxers!"

Zack was startled.

"Did I scare you?" teased Aliza, who had just woken up.

Zack just shook his head and put on the rest of his clothes.

Aliza grabbed a dress and stockings, then went into the bathroom to get washed up.

Aliza then came out with a gorgeous red silk dress and red stockings on with black shoes.

"Man, do I look under dressed," said Zack with a chuckle.

Aliza responded with a shrug of her shoulders not understanding why she only had nice dresses either.

After that, Zack and Aliza left outside to the school.

Zack and Aliza were in there fourth class sitting at a desk.

Zack was reading intently, as Aliza just flipped pages in the History of Lempton book.

Aliza sighed in bore.

"So your the chosen freak?" said a stranger evilly behind her.

The remark made Aliza angrily irritated. She turned to find a short fat girl looking at her with an evil smirk.

"What's with the look, freak. I just asked a question," said the girl.

Aliza became full of anger, as her eyes started to glow purple.

"Oh, getting mad," teased the girl evilly.

The girl turned and laughed, as she walked away with some other girls who were following her.

"What a jerk?" said Aliza, as she tried to shake off the agitation.

"I agree," said Zack, who was still starring into the History book.

Then the bell rang for lunch.

Aliza gathered her things from the other classes and got up.

As she headed for the door, the short fat girl came in the crowd and pushed her over.

Aliza fell straight on her butt.

"Are you okay?" said Zack behind her.

Another Lemption girl came over and helped Aliza on her feet.

"That's Becky the most popular junior student in school, but evil," she said.

Aliza looked at her confused.

"What makes her so popular?!" exclaimed Aliza angrily.

"Because of how impressive her Lemption transformation is," said Rebbeca.

"Yeah! Well it wouldn't impress me one bit! By the way who are you?" asked Aliza, as she let go of her anger.

"Oh, I'm sorry. My name is Rebecca Crytalyst. I'm a junior," said Rebecca, as she shook Aliza's hand.

Rebecca was twenty years old and had Black hair and Aqua colored furry ears with blue eyes.

She was wearing a blue dress.

"Hi, I'm Aliza and this is Zack. Thanks for helping me. Sorry, if I sounded rude to you at first," said Aliza.

"So why does Becky have a quarrel with, Aliza?" asked Zack.

"My guess is she doesn't want her popularity going to The Chosen One," said Rebecca.

"Oh, so that's why she's trying to make me look like a fool," said Aliza.

"So who were you paired up with?" asked Zack.

"Oh, Daniel. He's over there," said Rebecca.

Aliza saw a twenty year old good looking boy with brown ears and blond hair still sitting at a desk.

They came up to him.

Daniel looked up and had a stunned look on his face.

"You're...You're The...The...The Chosen One," he stuttered.

They introduced themselves and then headed to the lunch area.

The lunch room was a huge area with windows in the entire ceiling, like a full sun roof and windows all around, so there was no need for light.

Aliza and the others sat down at a one of the large lunch tables.

Zack and Daniel were eating some roast beef and gravy, while Aliza and Rebecca were sucking on a couple of popsicles.

"So how is it being The Chosen One," asked Rebecca.

"I don't really know. I mean till I came to this school I didn't even know I was The Chosen One," said Aliza.

"or my heritage for that matter," thought Aliza quietly to herself.

"Didn't your parents ever tell you?" asked Rebecca.

Aliza sat silent for a moment.

"I never knew my parents," said Aliza slowly.

"Oh...I'm sorry," said Rebecca sadly.

"Its okay," said Aliza.

"So how did you guys get together?" asked Daniel.

"We met when we were younger, then we moved away from Aliza's adoptive family. Recently, we found each other again and decided to be a couple," explained Zack.

"Wow," said Rebecca.

"So you got The Chosen One. What a babe to score...so did you get lucky yet, Zack," said Daniel with a chuckle.

SPLAT!!!

Rebecca broke her Popsicle all over Daniel's head.

"That's what you get for asking that," said Rebecca.

"Yuck!" said Daniel.

His hair and ears were full of sticky Popsicle juice pieces.

Aliza and Zack blushed and laughed quietly.

Then Aliza suddenly felt cold and heard ringing in her ears.

"Do you hear that?" asked Aliza suddenly.

They shook there heads.

Aliza suddenly fell to the ground paralyzed.

CRASH!!!

There were Vieniems above the lunchroom. The Vieniems broke through the sun roofs and then disappeared.

Students were screaming and being sliced and killed by the huge falling glass.

Aliza couldn't move and she looked horrified at the blood spilling from the bodies of dead students. She watched as Zack yelled at her, but heard nothing.

Aliza watched Zack pick her up and run to the nearest exist, as she layed in Zack's arms horrified and sweaty. Then she saw Principal Hartford run beside Zack into a hall.

Finally, she fainted.

Chapter 6

What are They in For?

Aliza opened her eyes and wasn't sure where she was.

"Are you alright?"

It was Zack.

Aliza jumped in Zack's arms and cried heavily.

"Shhh... we'll be alright. I know it was bad," said Zack.

He gently placed his arms around her and rubbed her back to try and comfort her.

"S...s...so many Le...Lemptions died, Zack. So many," cried Aliza.

Aliza dug her face into Zack's shoulder crying hysterically.

"Vieniems are evil creatures. Their instinct is to kill," said Zack gloomy.

"But Whhhhyyyy?" bursted Aliza in tears.

"It's okay. Were safe now? Shhh..." said Zack, as he tried to comfort her.

Zack felt a trobbing pain in his heart at the thought of the recent incident and felt even more sorry for Aliza. He knew Aliza must be feeling guilty because everyone said she was to protect the Lemptions from the Vieniems slaughter, but she couldn't do anything.

There was a knock at the door.

"Come in," called Zack.

It was Principal Hartford and another person, but a human.

"Thanks again for getting us out of there, Principal Hartford," said Zack.

Aliza was still crying profusely.

"Is she okay?" asked the human.

The human was an older man with long black hair

"It was a lot for her to go through," said Zack.

"It was quite an ordeal," grunted the human.

"Considering the attack was because the chosen one was present," said the Principal.

Aliza then bursted in loud tears on Zack's lap at the mention of her fault.

Zack's eyes glowed red and then gave the Principal a nasty look and growled at what he said.

"Oh sorry," said the Principal.

"Be careful of what you say, Hartford," said the human.

Aliza slowly began to settle down after a long while.

"Is...Is Rebecca and Daniel okay?" asked Aliza with a damp face.

"They came out behind us, after you fainted," said Zack.

"Why did I become paralyzed?" asked Aliza.

"Oh no, I was afraid of that," said the Principal with a gloom look.

"Afraid Of What!?" asked Zack angrily.

"Well... the transformation into a Lemption for Aliza will go in steps. How many, I don't know. But when she's in the presence of Vieniems, she won't be able to move or able to fight until she completes her full transformation," said the Principal.

"Why?" asked Zack.

"We're not really sure?" said the Principal.

"Who are you?" asked Aliza in dry eyes starring at the human leaning against the hallway's wall.

"His name is Brad. He's a skilled Vieniem hunter. He will protect the premises, while you're still transforming," explained Principle Hartford.

"Well...we are glad to see you're alright. We'll leave you so you can get some rest tonight," said Brad.

At that moment, they left out the door.

"Are you okay?" said Zack rubbing Aliza shoulders.

"Yeah...just shaken up," said Aliza, as she wiped away what was left of her tears.

She got up from under the covers and grabbed out a gown and underwear considering that it was late in the evening.

Zack suddenly bursted out laughing.

"What's the matter with you!" exclaimed Aliza with a weird look.

"LOOK AT YOU!" laughed Zack.

Aliza went to the bathroom stood in front of the full size mirror that was on the back of the bathroom door.

She looked normal and didn't see anything different.

Zack walked over and lifted the back of her skirt.

"What the heck are you doing?" yelled Aliza angered.

Suddenly, she was quite.

SWISH!

Aliza had a long white short-haired furry tail swishing back and forth.

"When they said transform, they weren't kidding," chuckled Zack.

They both laughed.

Then they got ready for bed and went to sleep; determined to let this whole event pass by.

Chapter 7

A Warning

Aliza and Zack just got in their Lemption Transformations class, while they and the students had frowns on their faces from the day before.

Aliza had on a yellow dress with a short skirt, so there was room for her new long tail.

Rebecca and Daniel were with them.

"I like your new tail, Aliza. It goes with your hair," said Rebecca.

"Do you like it yourself?" asked Daniel.

"Yeah...it's just sometimes I get this weird urge to chase it," said Aliza.

They laughed.

"Nice touch freak," said someone behind Aliza.

Aliza knew it was Becky and didn't care to look back.

"I saw you faint yesterday, scaredy cat. You don't deserve to be The Chosen One...freak," said Becky evilly.

Aliza was filling with anger at what she was saying and her eyes started to glow purple.

"Your parents would be so disappointed in you," said Becky slowly.

Aliza squeezed the book she was reading in anger, but never turned around.

"Look at me when I talk to you, Freak!" yelled Becky.

Aliza stayed turned.

Suddenly, Aliza felt a huge sharp pain at the end of her tail.

Becky stomped on it.

Aliza jumped up and turned around hissing with glowing eyes.

"Now did I get your attention?" teased Becky with an evil smirk.

"Your going to pay for that," said Aliza.

"Aliza Don't," said Zack.

Aliza shot him a look.

"Never mind," said Zack, as he backed off trembling at what look his wife gave him.

"I thought you were scared," tormented Becky.

Aliza's tail whipped strongly back and forth behind her.

"Think again," said Aliza angrily.

Suddenly, her tail hit the desk and it flew across the room and broke against the wall.

All the students backed away from the fight.

"Ooh...Freak is gonna hurt me," faked Becky.

"Witch!" growled Aliza.

"What! How dare you call me that?" yelled Becky.

At that, Becky grew claws and wiped her hand at Aliza's body.

Aliza leaped at an instant and supported her feet on two ceiling beams and used her tail for balance.

All the students yelled in amazement.

Becky looked up to find Aliza standing on the ceiling beams.

Aliza was amazed at what she did.

"Get down here, scaredy cat!" called Becky.

Aliza jumped and landed in front of Becky.

Suddenly, Aliza's nails grew into claws.

Becky whipped her claws at Aliza's head.

Aliza ducked, then ripped her claws at Becky's neck and just missed her.

Becky then tried to leap her claws at Aliza and Aliza disappeared.

Becky looked around to find her, but didn't see her.

Suddenly, Becky felt something curve around her neck tightly.

It was Aliza's tail.

Becky tried to relieve the pressure off her neck, but it was no use. Aliza's tail was to strong.

"Don't Ever Mess With Me Again," whispered Aliza into her ear behind her.

Then Aliza grabbed Becky by her neck with her claws and threw her to the ground.

Becky sat on the ground holding her neck. When she released her hand Becky had three cuts from Aliza's claws on her neck.

"I'll get you, Aliza," said Becky.

Becky got up, looked at Aliza in anger and ran out of the room.

Aliza's eyes stopped glowing and her claws disappeared.

"That was amazing!" exclaimed Zack.

Suddenly, Aliza became light headed and fell to the ground motionless.

She fainted.

Chapter 8

A Dark or Passionate Moment

Aliza awoke in their cottage laying on the bed.

"What...What happened?" asked Aliza.

She sat up a little light headed.

"You fainted," said Zack, who was sitting next to her.

Aliza looked across from her to see the Principal and, the Vieniem hunter, Brad.

"That was quite a fight you put up," said the Principal.

"You saw it!" exclaimed Aliza.

"Yes," he said.

"Why didn't you stop her?" asked Aliza.

"You see the girl you were fighting....what was her name...Becky. The real Becky was killed in that incident in the cafeteria," said the Principal sadly.

Zack and Aliza looked at each other speechless.

"Then who was she?" asked Zack.

"She was the leader of the Vieniem Clan, disguised as Becky," said Brad, who was leaning against the wall.

"She sure didn't put up much of a fight," said Aliza.

"My guess is she was testing you to see what a challenge you would be. And I liked the present you gave her on her neck. You sure taught her a lesson," said Brad.

"You were there too?" asked Aliza.

"I've always been around, but I give you guys privacy when you needed it. Such as a couple nights ago," said Brad.

He gave them a devious look and a smile.

"You didn't," said Zack.

"I did," he said.

Zack blushed.

Aliza got a chill down her back at the thought of him knowing what they did.

"Better hope you're not having cubs, Aliza," said Brad, as he laughed.

"SHUT UP...YOU PEEPING TOM!" growled Aliza.

Aliza was about ready to jump off the bed and tear him to shreds.

"Hey...I didn't watch. I said I gave you Privacy," said Brad.

"Doesn't give you any right to be poking your nose!" growled Aliza even more.

Zack was holding her back by her arms to prevent her from beating Brad senceless.

"OKAY! Let's Get Off The Subject," said the Principal.

"Why was he working so hard to be poking his nose in our window and following us around anyway?" asked Zack.

"You didn't tell them," said Brad, as he turned to the principal.

"Tell what?" asked Aliza.

Principal Hartford glanced from Aliza to the hunter for a moment.

"You see, Aliza. I wanted to wait for the right time to tell you. The Vieniem hunter...Brad...well...he's your Uncle Rain," said the Principal.

Zack's and Aliza's mouth hung wide open.

"How he's human!?" shouted Zack.

"Our dad was human and his wife was a Lemption. We were twins. Your dad was a Lemption and ...well...I was born a human, but we were still blood brothers," said Uncle Rain.

Aliza just stared at her Uncle with tears in her eyes.

"All this time you were alive! And...and...and you couldn't even say 'hi' to me or let me know that you were alive," yelled Aliza angrily.

She broke down crying in Zack's arms.

Zack gestured to them that it was time for them to leave.

Principle Hartford and Uncle Rain nodded in understanding and left from the cottage.

"Shhh...calm down ...it will be okay. I'm sure he didn't mean to remain so unknown to you. Remember...he's a Vieniem hunter. And Vieniem Hunters need to be very descret about their existence amungst others to be able to carry out their tasks," said Zack.

Aliza pulled herself up and dried her tears.

"It's just so sudden...all this," she said quietly.

Zack started to laugh.

"WHAT'S SO FUNNY!?" yelled Aliza.

She hit him hard in the side and knocked the wind out of him.

"It's just another something...happened earlier...while you were asleep," coughed Zack.

"What do you mean?" asked Aliza.

Zack was still trying to breath and just pointed to the bathroom mirror.

Aliza walked up to the mirror and just stood there stunned.

"I...I have tattoo's and different hair color...and fur," she said slowly.

Zack walked up to her, finally unclenching his stomach.

"Their called birth marks and they're very rare. And the fur is part of a Lemption's evolving," said Zack.

Aliza was unbelieving at the fur all over her body, face, and fluffy tail. Her tail and hair was a lighter purple with dark purple and white patterned fur all over her body. Then a dark blue diamond shaped crest embedded in the middle of her chest, just below her collar bone.

"What's this?" asked Aliza.

She ran her furry fingers across the crest.

"The principle explained while you were asleep, that the crest was born inside of you because you are The Chosen One. He said, it contains untold power," explained Zack.

"It's beautiful," said Aliza.

She looked at the crest in the mirror's reflection and felt a warm sensation flush over her.

Now she knew why she was called "The Chosen One."

The stone emitted a defining twinkling sparkle in the candle light.

Aliza went to bed with thoughts of how important it was for her to be strong.

Chapter 9

The Fight

Aliza and Zack were just coming from their History of Lempton class, walking through the school's picnic park. Other Lemptions were staring at Aliza's new transformation in wonder and amazement.

"Aliza! Zack! Hold up!" called someone behind them.

They turned to find that Principle Hartford was running to catch up with them. He had something in his hand and then he slowed to a stop trying to catch his breath.

"What do you want, Principle Hartford?" asked Aliza.

"I have something of you mothers and fathers for you," said Principle Hartford.

He opened his hand to reveal a black collar with a gold bell and a black leash with a gold latch.

"Uh, what is it?" asked Zack curiously.

The principle moved Aliza's hair to put the collar on, as he explained, "Your mother and father wore these before their wedding. These things will prove weather you two are compatible with one another, even though you two are still paired for life. And in your parent's time, these were a symbol of the male owning the female in marriage."

"What!" yelled Aliza angered.

The principle tightened the leash to Zack's wrist and left.

"Come on...it's not that bad," said Zack.

"Who Are You Kidding? YOU'RE NOT THE ONE OWNED BY ME," yelled Aliza, as she turned away from him in anger.

CLICK!

Aliza knew Zack just put the leash on her. Zack saw her turn with purple glowing eyes.

"I CAN'T BELIEVE YOU!" yelled Aliza.

She pulled away from him, using all her strength.

ALIZA AND ZACK

"Come on! Stop it!" said Zack from a distance.

Eventhough, Aliza pulled away from Zack the leash didn't keep them away for long. Suddenly, the leash acted like an elastic band and had them bounce back into each other's head and fall to the ground.

"Ouch!" said Aliza.

Aliza rubbed her head and got back up.

The whole park filled of students just watched.

Then Aliza started to drag Zack across the ground.

"Aliza! STOP!" yelled Zack.

Aliza stopped because she felt sorry for him.

Then Zack got up and said, "Come on, now you know how it goes in marriage."

Aliza got even more angered, slapped him, and started running.

Zack ran to try and keep up, "I didn't mean it, like that!"

Suddenly, a light pole got in between them.

CRASH!

Aliza and Zack smashed right into each other, because the leash got in the way.

Aliza layed on the ground with a horrible headache and said, "Okay, I give up!"

Zack got up and rubbed his head.

"When I said that...I didn't mean to say that I owned you in marriage. I meant to say that we would both be equal in marriage, because I love you," said Zack, as he said this he took the leash and went the other way around the pole, so the leash wouldn't be stuck.

Aliza's anger came to a halt, as she looked up into Zack's honest eyes. Zack smiled and jerked the leash, so Aliza would fall into his arms.

Aliza was frozen in her position, as Zack's head slowly came to hers and was about to kiss her.

Aliza's tail slowly curved around their bodies.

"So what are you doing?" teased Daniel.

Aliza jumped up and said, "uh nothing!"

"So where were you? We were worried about you?" said Rebecca.

"Yeah and nice new fur, Aliza. It's awesome," said Daniel.

After, Aliza got up and she brushed herself off, she said, "Yeah and check this out!"

Aliza showed them the dark blue crest in the middle of her chest, just below her collar bone.

"Is that the Chosen Stone?" asked Rebecca.

"Yeah." said Aliza.

Zack came by with Popsicles from an ice cream stand that just happened to be near the light pole where Aliza and Zack had their mishap, in the park for them. Apparently the leash stretched just long enough for Zack to reach it.

"So Zack, did you get lucky yet?" said Daniel with a smirk.

SPLAT!

Rebecca took all the popsicles from Zack's hands and smashed them all over Daniels head.

"Zack, you can't be giving weapons to my girl!" said Daniel, as he tried to pick out popsicle pieces from his hair and from his ears.

"Don't worry, as long as you don't say anything stupid. You're fine, Danny," assured Rebecca.

"So what is that?" asked Daniel, as he pointed to the leash and collar that was on Zack's wrist and Aliza's neck.

"Don't ask," said Aliza, who started to turn pink in the fur on her face and blushed.

Rebbecca and Daniel looked at each other with smiles on their faces and everyone in the park left to their next class, including Aliza, Zack, Daniel, and Rebbecca.

Chapter 10

How Did That Happen?
2 Weeks Later...

Aliza and Zack were getting dress for the First Quarter Dance Ceremony.

"You ready," said Zack.

Aliza had trouble putting on a beautiful red dress, as Zack had trouble putting on a handsome tuxedo because their leash and collar constantly got in the way.

"Okay, let's go," said Aliza.

Zack suddenly grabbed her arm, "Wait! I have something for you."

Zack sat her on the bed and he got on one knee. Then he took a green velvet box out of his pocket and held it in front of her.

Aliza held her breath at the hope of knowing what it was.

He opened it to reveal a Diamond studded opal heart with a gold circle around it, and an earring connection.

Aliza frowned a little.

"You don't like it," said Zack sadly.

"No! No! It's n...not that, it's just ...ummm...shouldn't be a ring. I'm Sorry!" said Aliza.

Zack just laughed and put the earring in her left ear.

"No, It's okay. It's understandable... Lemption's marry with and earring for the left ear, not a ring for the left index finger," explained Zack, as he spoke he pinned the earring to Aliza's ear.

"It Hurts," said Aliza.

"It might for a while...but the pain will go away in a few minutes," said Zack.

"Oh Zack! Thank you!" said Aliza, as she jumped on him with a great big hug.

Then Zack and Aliza walked out onto the sun set lit stone path to the school. Aliza looked lovingly into Zack's eyes. Aliza loved what the sun set lighting did to his red hair. Zack, in return, smiled and put his arm around Aliza. They both fell happily in love for each other.

CLICK! SNAP!

Suddenly, the leash and collar fell off Zack's wrist and Aliza's neck.

Aliza and Zack looked at each other and laughed.

"Well...now we know we're compatible. Took long enough it must have a malfunction." chuckled Aliza.

Zack picked up the collar, moved Aliza's hair, and slowly put it back on her neck, "But I like this on you. It looks cute with your dress...and even cuter with your birthmarks."

"Awe...you're sweet, but..." said Aliza.

Suddenly, she picked up the leash and clicked it on her collar. Then she tightened the leash on Zack's wrist.

Zack looked confused.

"Remember you own me," teased Aliza with a wink.

Zack went along with Aliza's flirting and suddenly started to tickle Aliza. Aliza bursted out laughing and ran with Zack close behind her to the school for the First Quarter Dance.

The dance was being held for the night because Vieniems had not shown up since the last attack.

Aliza stopped behind a crowd of students in the ballroom and Zack grabbed her by the waist, picked her up, and started twirling her around in circles.

Then the leash and collar came off again and Zack quickly slipped it in his pocket.

Aliza's laughs were so loud, that the whole student body turned to watch.

"Look's like you guys are having fun," said Rebecca, as she came around with Daniel.

Aliza's and Rebecca's dress looked exactly identical and so did Zack's and Daniel's tuxes'.

"Hey, can you guys sing," asked Rebecca into the microphone.

REBBECA

Zack looked at Aliza with a smile.

"Sure," said Aliza.

Aliza and Zack followed Rebecca and Daniel on the stage.

Aliza looked at the crowd of dancing students below who were watching them.

"Just follow my lead," said Rebecca.

Aliza swallowed with a knot in her stomach, as Daniel passed Zack and her both a microphone.

"OKAY EVERYONE READY TO ROCK. THE CHOSEN ONE A.K.A. ALIZA AND HER BOY HAS OFFERED TO SING WITH US TONIGHT!" called Rebecca.

There was a loud cheer that followed.

Then the music started.

"We are girls. Nothing ever can. Get to our clan," sung Aliza and Rebecca, as they put their backs together.

Suddenly, Zack and Daniel snatched them both, and sung, "We are boys. In the dark of night. We will bite."

Suddenly, Aliza felt a lurch in her stomach and stopped following Rebbecca's singing.

She quickly gestured to shut the music off and turned quickly to Zack, "I have to see the nurse NOW!"

Aliza collapsed to her knees, because of the pain in her stomach.

Zack swooped Aliza up in his arms and ran down the steps through the crowd, as Rebecca and Daniel followed.

They ran to the nurse's office.

"Has she eaten anything lately?" asked the nurse.

She was giving Aliza some pain killer and taking blood.

Later, Aliza was in a gown waiting for results in a patient room with Rebecca, Daniel, and Zack.

Then there was a knock at the door and the nurse came in with a file.

"Aliza," she said.

"What's wrong with her?" asked Zack with an almost crying expression.

"Nothing......your wife is expecting," said the Nurse with a smile.

Zack laughed and everyone looked at him with an odd expression.

Aliza was stunned, her Uncle Rain jinxed her.

"Pregnant, she...she's not pregnant!" laughed Zack.

The nurse stared him down seriously.

Zack slowly stopped laughing starring back at the nurse.

"Pregnant," said Zack.

He slowly began to realize the situation.

THUD!

Zack passed out cold onto the floor.

Chapter 11

Another Day

Zack just layed next Aliza on their bed in their cottage and stared at the ceiling. He couldn't believe he was going to be a father.

"Zack...are you there? You'll be fine as a father," said Aliza, as she woke up.

Some how she knew he was up all night.

Aliza got out of the bed and went to her clothes dresser.

"Are you sure the nurse didn't make mistake about you being pregnant?" asked Zack hopefully.

"I don't think so. Now get up, we have to go see Uncle Rain. He said he had something for us," said Aliza.

"You mean he has something for you, Aliza. He said its stuff from your parents, not mine," said Zack.

Zack stretched, slowly got up, and left to change in the bathroom.

When Aliza and Zack were done, they came out and looked at each other with a smile. Zack walked up to Aliza and slowly put his arms around her.

"You're going to be a mother," said Zack, as he looked with a smile into Aliza's eyes.

"Girl or boy?" asked Aliza.

"I don't know, but I bet it'll be amazing. But we do have to think of names," said Zack.

Zack finally embraced the thought of having a child... having spent all night thinking how he would be as a father.

Then they started heading out the door.

"How about Kiesa for a boy, and Joe for a girl," said Aliza.

"I don't think so....I always liked Lily for a girl. This may sound corny, but lilies are my favorite flower," said Zack.

"Awe...That's sweet," said Aliza.

"I just don't know how I'll tell my parents," said Zack.

They laughed, but Zack choked a little in his chuckle at the end with a knot in his stomach.

Aliza and Zack started walking along the stone path and saw another Lemption who was dressed almost as a gothic and looked to be twenty years old. They saw him walk into a house covered with flowers and garden decorations that were all over the house.

"Creepy guy," said Zack.

Then the Lemption turned toward Zack and spit on the ground with a growl and continued to the cottage.

The Lemption had green eyes, black hair, and pale green ears.

"Scary," said Aliza.

"You think," said Zack with a chuckle.

The word "Shastekae" was written all over the cottage in flowers.

"That must be his name," said Aliza.

"Talk about obsessed," said Zack.

Suddenly, a Lemption girl came running out of the cottage.

"Shastekae, I made your favorite muffins," she said.

"Come on, Sweetheart Lemry... let's go inside," said Shastekae with a growl.

He slammed the door.

"Pretty name," said Aliza with a weird face.

"Let's get going," said Zack.

Then they started walking through the cottages.

"Uncle Rain! Are you there!?" called Aliza, as she opened a large wooden door.

Aliza and Zack came in, and looked around. Everything looked like nothing had been touch in years. Books were tied with cob webs and old wooden toys for children were everywhere.

Suddenly, they heard the voice of Uncle Rain.

"Hold on a minute I have it here some where!" called Uncle Rain.

Aliza was curious to what he had for her.

Suddenly, there was a thud around the corner and dust clouded.

Uncle Rain came out coughing with a large shoe box in his arms.

"Here...this might interest you, Aliza," said Uncle Rain, as he set the box on the table.

Aliza and Zack sat at an old wooden table in the middle of the dusty room.

Aliza slowly opened the box and was stunned.

She pulled out photos of a woman Lemption. The woman looked almost exactly the same as Aliza, but had blue hair and pink ears. Aliza also found that the woman Lemption was wearing the same marriage collar Aliza had worn.

"Is this?" asked Aliza slowly.

"Yep...that's your mom," said Uncle Rain with a smile.

She couldn't believe how beautiful her Mom was.

"Wow...She's Sexy!" said Zack.

SMACK!

Aliza slapped him for what he said.

Uncle Rain laughed.

"I mean, she looks just like you," said Zack, as he rubbed his face.

Aliza growled.

Then she picked up a scroll that had a gem on a collar wrapped around it with the name on the collar Reinstone Crystal.

"What's this?" asked Aliza.

"That's something your father gave his life up for while protecting your mother, while she was pregnant with you," said Uncle Rain.

Aliza's heart dropped.

"How do you know?" asked Aliza.

"I was there," said Uncle Rain.

Aliza became sad with tear filled eyes.

"What happened?" asked Zack.

Uncle Rain turned down his lamp, got up, looked out the window, and closed the curtain.

Then Uncle Rain sat back down and began to explain.

"It was a stormy night... your mother, I, and your father were on a mission for the first Principal of the Lemptions. Your mom followed along because they had to protect you inside her because you were to be the The Chosen One. We were to retrieve the sacred scroll and powerful Reinstone crystal from The Vieniem Leader's castle. We were in one of the caves on the mountain perches for the Vieniem leader's minions. Your mother was preparing a meal, while we went to steal the scroll. When we came back your mother was under attack by the Vieniem leader and her minions. Your father and I fought off as many as we could. Then the Vieniem leader got to your mother. She said, 'I'll have your Child as my own!' Your mother scratched her up good till the contractions started in the middle of the fight. As soon as the Vieniem Leader had her chance, she sliced part of your Mom's belly and started to bleed

immensely. I ran over and released the light of the Rein stone at them and the Vieniem leader and her minions left. Then your father turned to aid your mother and one of the minions grabbed your father, while he was distracted and bit him and he tried to fight it off . But by the time the venom started to take affect the Vieniem dropped him off the cliff of the mountain. It was too late to save him and when I turned back to your mother. She was almost dead. When I pulled you from her…her last words were, 'Save her, protect her, and tell her that we love her.' And this scroll hides the key to the future of the Lemptions and only the chosen one should yield this crystal," explained Uncle Rain.

"How did you know she was to be The Chosen One?" asked Zack.

"Because her Mom had the symbols of the ancient Lemption language, as birthmarks on her back, while her pregnancy. They were the sign of the Chosen One's birth," explained Uncle Rain.

Aliza looked down with tears pouring down her face.

Suddenly, she became angry and furious with purple and glowing eyes.

Then Aliza suddenly looked straight at her Uncle Rain.

Then Aliza got up and started hitting Uncle Rain with the scroll and her fist with all her force screaming, "YOU COULD HAVE DONE SOMETHING!!! YOU COULD HAVE DONE SOMETHING!!! I HATE YOU!!! I HATE YOU!!! YOU DIDN'T EVEN TAKE ME IN!!! I HATE YOU!!!"

Zack pulled her off of Uncle Rain with all his strength. Then Aliza ran out of the cottage crying hysterically.

Zack then pulled Uncle Rain to his feet.

"Are you okay?" asked Zack breathing heavily.

"I'm okay. She's a strong girl," said Uncle Rain with a difficult chuckle.

"I'm sorry, she's been kind of emotional lately," said Zack.

"It's okay. I'm more worried about her. That was a lot for her to take in. She'll understand soon. She'll read letters and see photos. What will hopefully set her mind at ease. Take this now and go comfort her...GO!" said Uncle Rain.

Uncle Rain handed him the box.

Zack went to the door and turned around to say sorry again.

"Don't say another word! Now GO!" said Uncle Rain with two back eyes, proving that he took a beating.

Zack ran out of door to their cottage with the shoe box in his arms and followed Aliza.

Chapter 12

An Upset!

"Aliza! Aliza!" called out Zack, as he entered their cottage.

He heard her crying.

CRASH!

SMASH!

Zack walked through broken plates that crunched under his feet in the hallway.

Then suddenly a plate came right for him.

CRASH!

It just missed him and broke against the wall.

"Hey, Watch It!" yelled Zack, as he came into the bedroom where Aliza was.

"Leave me alone," sniffed Aliza, as she sat down on the bed.

Zack looked down at the broken plates. He didn't know that the news would be this hard for her.

Then he looked at Aliza and saw blood trailing down her right hand and legs.

He dropped the box next to the bed and zoomed into the closet in the bathroom to get bandages and a cloth. Then he wetted it in the sink and went straight to Aliza.

"Aliza, Are You Crazy!? You could bleed to death," said Zack, as he wrapped the wet cloth around her hand.

She sighed in pain.

"I cut it, while throwing the plate pieces. I'm sorry...it's just," apologized Aliza.

Zack saw Aliza pouring tears and he was no longer angry. Then he wrapped and fastened the bandage on her hand.

"Thank goodness the cut isn't that bad!" thought Zack to himself.

"I'm sorry...I almost hit you," choked Aliza still tearing.

"Don't worry about it," said Zack, as he held her close. He kissed her head.

"It will be okay," said Zack.

"I just can't believe it," said Aliza.

"Why don't you get some rest, while I clean up in here," said Zack, as he layed her down and pulled the blanket over her.

"Thank you," said Aliza.

"For what?" said Zack, as he turned around.

"For being there for me, when I need you most," said Aliza softly.

"That's what I'm here for," said Zack.

She smiled and closed her eyes.

Zack saw her tail wrap around her and his eyes softened in care.

Chapter 13

A Rude Awakening

Aliza awoke from her sleep to find a clean cottage.

"Zack?" called Aliza.

"Right here. I'm just taking out the trash," said Zack, as he came out from the corner.

Suddenly, there was a knock at the door.

"Who's That?" asked Aliza.

Then Aliza and Zack went for the door.

When Zack opened it they saw that Principal was standing there with a smile on his face.

"What the matter, Principal Hartford?" asked Aliza.

"I have some good news, Zack," said Principal Hartford happily.

"Really What?" asked Zack excited.

"Your parents have come for a visit," said the Principal.

THUD!

Zack passed out cold on the floor with the trash bag laying on top of him.

"What's the matter with him?" asked the Principle.

"I think it's because he hasn't told his parents about me being pregnant," said Aliza, as she shook her head.

"Oh my," said the Principle.

"Yeah...I'll get some water," said Aliza, as she turned to the kitchen.

Aliza came back with a small cup of water and poured it on Zack's face.

He woke up with a start.

"Come on. Your parents are waiting, Zack," said the Principle with a frown.

Zack frowned.

They followed the principle to the school and came to a small room.

"Zacky Poo!" called his Mom.

She gave him a huge hug.

Zack turned red in embaressement at the mention of his mom's nickname for him.

She had blue ears and blond hair and his Dad had black ears and black hair.

His Dad was sitting in a chair with a smile.

"So you must be, Aliza. We're so happy The Chosen One would be our daughter-in-law," said his Mom.

She gave Aliza a big hug.

"I'm James and this is Lisa," said Zack's Dad, James.

"Hi, Mom. Hi, Dad," said Aliza with a corny smile.

Zack sat down slowly with an uncomfortable feeling in his stomach.

"I brought you some sugar cookies," said Lisa.

She pulled out a huge plate of cookies.

"I'm not hungry," said Zack, as he held his stomach in agony.

Aliza started scarfing down the cookies two at a time with no hesitation.

"I know you guys are already husband and wife, but do you plan on having a wedding. Oh, I hope so," said Lisa excitedly.

"I don't know," said Zack, as he rubbed his neck in guilt.

Suddenly, all you could hear was the sound of Aliza's munching.

"Look...I have something to tell you," choked Zack.

He looked over at Aliza, who was covered with crumbs.

She had finished the whole plate of cookies.

"Gees girl, you eat like your having a baby cub," said Lisa with a laugh.

"A newborn?" asked Aliza, still with stuffed cheeks.

"Uh huh," chuckled Lisa.

Zack coughed and choked.

"What's wrong, son?" said James with a frown.

"Can I use the bathroom?" said Zack, as he got up.

"NO! Sit Down!" said James firmly.

"Do you have something to tell us, Zacky?" said Lisa slowly.

"Ummm...She's......Pregnant." said Zack slowly with a frowning chuckle.

"WHAT!!!" yelled both of Zack's parents.

"I can't believe you, Zacky," yelled his Mom.

"Come On, Honey. Let's Go. We told him to wait, till after a real wedding. Let's give him time to think about what he's done," said James angrily.

Suddenly Lisa turned to Aliza and whispered to her, "Don't worry. It was Zacky's fault. Well have a baby shower later."

She winked to Aliza.

"Ouch!"

James hit Zack hard on the head.

The door slammed behind them.

"Well...that could have gone worse," said Aliza with a chuckle, as she brushed off the crumbs.

Zack made a stupid smile, while he rubbed his head.

Chapter 14

Professor Flibbinabber Revealed

4 Months Later...

Aliza and Zack started their Lemption Math class and began working on their third unit assignment.

Suddenly, Zack recognized the face under the hat and behind the glasses of the class's teacher.

Then Zack leaned in for a better look at Professor Flibbinabber because he looked familiar.

Professor Flibbinabber was facing the class explaining Lemption algebra equations from the chalk board.

The Professor was wearing a black out fit with a long cape like jacket with a tall collar.

Suddenly, a piece of chalk snapped Zack right between the eyes.

"You Jerk!" yelled Zack angrily.

The class suddenly watched and listened intently.

"Now continue your lesson or detention," ordered the Professor angrily, as he turned to the chalkboard in an instant.

Suddenly, a Lemption girl ran in the classroom with a lunch bag.

"Your lunch, sweetie. You forgot it," called the girl, as she ran up to Professor Flibbinabber.

Suddenly, the Professor snapped the chalk in half on the board with a weird expression.

He turned slowly.

"Honey....ummm....why are you here? You're not supposed to be," choked the Professor.

The class started giggling.

"What did you say I forgot?" choked the professor.

"Your lunch, Shastekae. And guess what? I baked your favorite chocolate cupcakes and put your name on them. Then I sprinkled them with rainbow sprinkles. Just the way you like them," she said sweetly.

Suddenly, his hand crushed the chalk to dust.

"Oh....noooo," whispered Shastekae to himself.

Suddenly, the classroom bursted out laughing.

"Hi, my name is Sweetheart Lemry. Yeah! He loves homework...especially math. He's really good at it. That's why the Principle made him a teacher," said Sweetheart happily.

"Not helping, Sweetheart...I'll give you a kiss, if you don't say anymore," said Shastekae.

Sweetheart blushed with a smile because Shastekae wasn't the lovey dovey type.

Sweetheart was twenty years old and had silver ears, white hair, and pink eyes. She was wearing a pink dress with white frills on the end of the skirt and puffed sleeves.

"Ahhh...nice...she gave away your secret," said Zack angrily.

"Hey, so you're the reason I've been getting F's, isn't it. A student shouldn't be in charge of that," said Daniel angered.

"No...That was your fault. You gave idiotic answers. Even my wife's cat could do better," said Shastekae.

"Don't you insult my friend!" said Zack.

Daniel and Zack transformed ready to fight.

Shastekae shooed Sweetheart as much as he could to the other side of the room.

Daniel pounced on Shastekae's desk.

Daniel was a large twelve foot cat-like werewolf with brown fur, blond leopard-like patterns, and bronze eyes.

Shastekae suddenly turned around and transformed.

His body was much larger then both Daniel's and Zack's transformations by a foot and a half.

Shastekae had large and sharp black claws, black fur, and a large bushy tail.

He also had pale green patterns on his fur and saber like fangs.

The pale green intimidated Daniel, because it was the color of Vieniem's skin.

"Dude, he's part Vieniem," whispered Daniel to Zack.

"That's ridiculous. It's just a color," growled Zack.

Zack readied himself to pounce.

"Let's fight then," said Shastekae, as he let his claws out even longer.

Zack jumped and dug his teeth into Shastekae's leg.

Shastekae let out a howl of pain and the earth shook.

"His howl causes earthquakes," said Daniel shaking.

The class backed away.

Daniel swallowed his fright and pounced to Shastekae.

Shastekae then grabbed a hold of Zack's tail and threw him into Daniel.

"Nice tail...Makes you look feminine," teased Shastekae.

"You should talk!" spoke Zack angrily, as he got onto his hind legs.

Aliza and Rebecca watched horrified at what their husbands were doing.

Shastekae lashed out his claws at Zack and he jumped out of the way.

Then Daniel bit his arm and Shastekae shook him off, while doing so,

Shastekae used his tail and threw Daniel into the wall by his neck.

"Stop Please!" yelled Sweetheart from the doorway.

Shastekae stopped and looked sorrowfully at his crying mate.

Suddenly, Zack and Daniel got their chance and pounced on him.

They slashed there claws.

Shastekae ripped out patches of their fur, as they continued to scratch him up.

Then Daniel grabbed a desk and raised it above his head.

He tried to hit Shastekae, but he was too quick. Shastekae took the desk in Daniel's arms and broke it on his head.

Daniel was dazed and wobbled on his feet.

"Stop Please!" yelled Sweetheart again.

Shastekae looked at her and punched Zack in the face one last time and dropped him to the floor.

"Stop Please!" cried Sweetheart again.

Zack picked himself up.

"Shut Up, You Witch!" yelled Zack to Sweetheart.

Shastekae backed away quickly from the fight and detransformed. He shook in fear, as he watched Sweetheart's red face because he knew what was going to happen next.

Sweetheart transformed furious and angry.

She transformed into a huge ten foot cat-like werewolf with white fur and pink eyes.

"What did you say?" said Sweetheart in a furious growl.

Suddenly, her eyes turned red and her fur turned pink in anger. Her tail swung wildly.

"You shouldn't have said that," said Daniel in a pitiful voice.

Zack nodded his head in fear.

Her tail lashed for Daniel.

CRASH!

He landed face first in the trash can so hard it knocked him unconscious and detransformed.

Zack tried to run, but Sweetheart grabbed his tail and swirled him in the air into the chandelier above the math class.

Zack detransformed tangled in the chandelier.

Sweetheart detransformed and breathed heavily.

"You Never Say That To A Lady!" said Sweetheart in a grunting growl.

Then she grabbed Shastekae by the ear and pulled him with her.

"Class Dismissed!" Shastekae tried to say with pain.

Rebecca was furious because of her Daniel's stupid behavior.

Aliza looked up at Zack angrily.

"You idiot," said Aliza with her arms folded.

Zack shrugged his shoulders, while he hung on the chandelier with a black eye.

Suddenly, he fell to the ground and accidently pulled the fire alarm with his foot, while layed on the ground being soaked by the sprinklers.

Aliza buried her face in her hands embarrassed.

The principle walked right in front of Sweetheart's and Shastekae's way, as he shook his head with a frown.

"Nurse, then Detention the three of you! NOW!" said Principle Hartford with a growl.

Suddenly, Daniel picked his head off the ground, still with the trash can on it.

"What's going on?" asked Daniel.

"OOOUCH!"

Rebecca gave Daniel a good kick in the butt.

"AHHHH!"

Then she punched the garbage can on his head, which ringed in his ears.

Everyone just shook their head and evacuated the room.

Chapter 15

The Dungeon Dudes

"Now you guys get in here and stay here. Your wives will stay with the nurse. I'll pick you up, when you've learned to be civilized Lemptions." said Principle Hartford angrily.

As he said this, he placed chained iron cuff s around their wrists.

Ouch!

The cuffs weight had Daniel fall to the ground.

"What About SWEETHEART!?" asked Zack immediately.

"Yeah!?" asked Daniel, just as upset.

"She had the right, from what she told me. I can't believe your mouth, Zack. Aliza wasn't too happy about it either," said the Principle disgusted.

"Good for Sweetheart," said Shastekae sarcastically.

Zack swallowed in guilt because of his words in front of his wife, Aliza.

The Principle left the Dungeon and slammed the big wooden door behind him.

They found themselves in an old medieval torture chamber with skulls, chains, and broken bones everywhere.

They sat at three moldy stone desks bolted to the ground in the middle of a bone heap.

There was a long wait.

"You're such a kiss up to the principle for being a teacher," said Daniel upset.

"Yeah, WHO would agree to that," said Zack to Shastekae.

"Well...it was either that or fail Lemption chemistry. And I want to get into Lemption college," said Shastekae honestly.

"There's no Lemption college for us, you idiot," said Daniel.

Zack and Daniel laughed.

Then Zack turned to Shastekae hoping for a chuckle and found him silent and sad.

"I was hoping for a college of my own," said Shastekae with a frown.

Zack and Daniel stopped laughing.

"I watched other kids go to school, while I lived alone on the streets," said Shastakae sadly.

"Where were your parents?" asked Zack with a frown.

Shastekae looked down and a tear fell from his eye and shook his head.

"You don't know?" asked Zack slowly.

"No," said Shastekae with a sad expression on his face.

"Is that your dream, Shastekae?" asked Daniel slowly.

"Yes," Shastekae put simply.

Daniel and Zack looked at each other silently.

They finally put aside their differences.

"Sooo...Shastekae...that's a cute girl you scored," said Daniel, as he tried to cheer up Shastekae.

Shastekae laughed.

"I know, but she's kind of annoying," said Shastekae with a chuckle.

"You know, she's a keeper. ..but Aliza, She's to emotional," said Zack cheerfully.

"You're kidding right! But you scored big! She's THE CHOSEN ONE!!!" said Daniel in a funny awe.

Shastekae turned to Zack with a devious smile on his face.

"I actually thought Aliza was sexy hot," said Shastekae.

Daniel laughed, "You're right."

Zack growled.

"Hey! You talk about your women, not mine," said Zack angrily.

"You brought it up, Zack," said Daniel.

They laughed.

Suddenly, the door knob on the door of the dungeon unlocked and turned.

The door opened and the Principle came in with a smile.

"SOOOO you finally came to your senses," said Principle Hartford.

"YES!" they said.

"Get me outta here...it's sooo creepy," said Daniel with a cold shiver.

"Well, let's hope you don't need to come back here," said the Principal.

They nodded their heads.

"Your wives are waiting at the park. I told them to put it behind them, to save you guys some trouble. I can't guarantee it though," said Principal Hartford, as he led them up the stairs.

"Thanks!" said Zack knowing he'll probably be in for it anyways.

"Also, you're all invited to my wedding!" said Shastekae.

"I'll have to let you borrow something before that happens. I'll give it to you before the dance tonight," said Zack with a chuckle.

"Really, what's that?" asked Shastekae.

"Ooooh...nothing. You'll find out," said Zack with a crude smile.

They all came out into the park, as the principle left them for dead.

"What do you think of the dress Aliza let me borrow, Shastekae?" asked Sweetheart.

When Shastekae looked at her, he was stunned. Her thighs were curved with just a slight peak at the end of the slit of her dress. Then the magenta lines and strings following the pink silk of the dress brought out her eyes and her fair skin.

He had flutters rise in his stomach.

"You...You're gorgeous," he said.

She winked with her face and her beautifully braided hair hidden behind a flower.

THUD!

Shastekae tripped on a rock because he was distracted by her beauty.

Aliza and Rebecca laughed, as he got up and brushed himself off .

"It's good to see you getting along," said Aliza, as she shook her head at Zack.

Zack looked to the ground.

"Well here... we have an ultrasound picture," said Aliza, as she handed him the sheet.

"Wh....why...why is there two heads?" asked Zack in a panic.

"Their twins," said Aliza cheerfully.

Zack made a wobbly smile and fell backwards.

THUD!

He passed out cold in the grass.

Chapter 16

The Talalabata Death Dance

Aliza got out of the bathroom in the dress she received the first day she came to the school.

"Why are you wearing this again? There's so many other dresses I haven't seen you in," said Zack with a smile.

Aliza laughed.

"I don't know.....it's special. And since we're nearing the end of the semester, it resembles what we started together," said Aliza meaningfully.

Zack turned slowly with a smile and walked up close to her.

"You know...I never got to thank you," said Zack, as he smiled handsomely.

"For what?" asked Aliza.

"For accepting me as your mate," said Zack surely.

"And how do you expect to thank Me," said Aliza with a flirtatious smile.

Zack suddenly took her head to his and kissed her.

Aliza felt a sensation run through her whole body from her finger tips to her toes.

They embraced each other for a long moment and then headed out the door.

"Hold on. I almost forgot something," said Zack.

He opened a drawer and pulled out the leash and collar that they had recieved from Principle Hartford.

"Who's that for?" laughed Aliza.

"Well Shastekae and Sweetheart are getting married and I figured since we had to go through it. Well...it might be exciting for them," said Zack with a devious smile.

Aliza just shook her head at him with a crude smile.

Then they headed out to the group of Sweetheart, Shastekae, Daniel, and Rebecca.

"I have it, Shastekae!" called Zack, as he and Aliza were walking down the stone path.

When Zack reached the group Shastekae looked in his hand and stood hesitantly.

"Wha...what's that?" asked Shastekae.

He was scared of what would happen next.

"Here Sweetheart...me and Aliza used this to see if we were compatible with each other," said Zack, as he shoved the leash and collar into Sweetheart's hands before she could react.

"I don't like this idea," said Shastekae slowly.

SNAP! CLICK!

Sweetheart already had the collar on Shastekae and the leash around her wrist.

"Uh, Sweetheart...that's not how it works." said Aliza with an awkward smile.

Zack bursted out laughing instantly.

Daniel and Rebecca made quiet giggles.

"I HATE YOU!" exclaimed Shastekae, as he shook his head at Zack.

Shastekae turned red in embarrassment.

"Come on, Baby. Let's go," said Sweetheart giddy-like.

GAG! CHOKE! GAG! GAG!

She yanked hard on the leash and pulled hard on Shatekae's neck.

"Just wait till I get off this leash, Zack! I'll kill you!" yelled Shastekae.

Zack still laughed hysterically.

THUD!

Shastekae fell to the ground because Sweetheart was pulling to hard.

DRAAAAAG!

Shastekae was being dragged and just layed there brushing along the ground holding onto the leash with all his strength to avoid being strangled.

"OH BROTHER!!!" thought Shastekae.

They all walked to the ballroom and through gardens, while Shastekae was still being dragged.

He couldn't get up because Sweetheart was still pulling to hard.

"HONEY....PLEASE STOP...**YOUR GOING TO RIP MY HEAD OFF!**" screamed Shastekae from the top of his lungs.

Then they walked into a ballroom full of nicely dressed Lemptions and started dancing.

The ballroom was huge with large windows all around the room. The windows were open because it was a nice cool evening.

Suddenly, Principle Hartford came by the group.

"So are you kids having fun?" he asked.

"I'm not." said Shastekae.

Sweetheart was twirling him around in the leash, laughing like it was some sick game.

Shastekae thought to himself, "I wonder if she'll stop if I give her a kiss. MAN!"

Shastekae didn't like the idea, but quickly grabbed Sweetheart's head and kissed her on the lips.

Sweetheart giggled.

"You don't give her kisses very often do you?" asked Daniel because he noticed Shastekae's bothered look.

"No," said Shastekae quietly.

Sweetheart jumped with joy and twirled.

SLAM! THUD!

Sweetheart twirled into Shastekae and fell to the floor tangled in the leash.

"You Moran," said Shastekae with a smile.

Sweetheart made a silly giggle and goofy smile.

CLICK!

The leash and collar finally came off .

"Man, it took us longer to loose the collar and leash," said Zack.

"Yeah...and you know what else you're going to loose, Zack," said Shastekae.

"What?" asked Zack.

"**YOUR LIFE!**" yelled Shastekae.

Shastekae immediately got up and started beating Zack to the ground.

THUD! BOOM! BANG! SLAM! BANG! CRASH! BOOM!

"Principle Hartford, stop them!" shouted the girls, as other lemptions starred at Shastekae's and Zack's actions.

Daniel just watched the fight with a funny smile.

"Sorry, but I Think Shastekae is in the right," said Principle Hartford, as he shook his head with a smile.

The girls gave the dasterdly principle a horrified look.

Principle Hartford knew another fight would eventhoughly break out between the boys and couldn't wait to bring them to detention, which apparantly he enjoyed doing.

CRASH!

Suddenly, Vieniems flocked through the windows.

Many Lemptions ran for their lives, but some stayed to fight.

Aliza felt a rush of cold up her spine.

Suddenly, she fell to the floor motionless.

She heard nothing, but saw Vieniems fighting the students strongly.

She watched as Shastekae, Rebecca, Daniel, Sweetheart, and Zack fought to keep the Vieniems off her.

Suddenly, she saw a Vieniem take hold of Zack's leg and bite it.

Her heart stopped.

She watched in horror as he struggled to fight it off. She saw him detransform and turn pale, as the Venom started to take effect.

Suddenly, Shastekae came in, jumped in the air, twirled, and bashed his foot and hind claws into the Vieniem's head.

It released and flew off in pain.

Zack took the last of his strength and crawled beside Aliza.

Aliza was horrified at the look in his sorrow and tear filled eyes.

He was pale, in pain, and had only a few seconds of life left.

She looked in his eyes, but didn't want to believe what she was seeing.

Finally, she watched him mouth the words "I Love You" with a weak smile and a tear fell from his eye.

Then his eyes closed slowly and his body layed lifeless.

Aliza suddenly grew hot with anger and she felt herself get up off the ground.

The fighting around her suddenly stopped.

She had her final transformation before everyone's eyes and the Vieniems became frightened.

She grew white feathery wings and her purple patterns disappeared. She had white fur covering her whole body. Her hair turned to a light lilac purple and she grew long white fangs and claws. She grew five times bigger than any normal Lemption transformation.

Suddenly, she let out a deafening howl and scream of anger and frustration.

Then clear crystals shot forth from the ground and emitted blinding light.

The Vieniems scattered in fear, running, and flying into each other trying to squeeze threw the windows to many at a time.

When the Vieniems were gone the crystals faded back into the ground and didn't hurt any of the other Lemption students.

Suddenly, Aliza detransformed, ran, and kneeled beside Zack's lifeless body.

She was crying heavily, as everyone else watched in tears.

She slowly stroked Zack's hair.

"I'm sorry, Zack. I'm sorry. I wasn't there to save you...to help you win the fight. I...I couldn't move," cried Aliza.

When Aliza looked outside, she noticed it was raining.

Suddenly, she bursted yelling in tears and shook Zack's body.

"Wake Up! Wake Up, Zack! Don't Be Dead! Please Don't!" she yelled.

Then she layed her head on his chest to see if she could hear a heartbeat, but she heard nothing.

When she felt his hand and it was cold as ice.

She didn't want to believe it that her husband was dead.

"No...No...No. You didn't even get to see our children," she said softly.

She laid herself on his chest and cried heavily.

"I'm sorry," she whispered.

Suddenly, Aliza felt a kind hand on shoulder and turned around.

It was Rebecca.

"It's not your fault." said Rebecca.

"Isn't there something we can do?" asked Aliza.

She looked up at Principle Hartford with watery eyes.

"Maybe we can bring him to the nurse...but I don't think she'll be able to do anything," said the Principle sadly.

Shastekae kindly picked up Zack's lifeless body in a gut guilt feeling and they ran to the nurse. Shastekae didn't mean for his words to actually come true.

Chapter 17

A Hopeless Case

Shastekae layed Zack slowly on a hospital bed and the nurse came in.

As soon as, she saw Zack's body her smile turned into a frown.

"Oh no! Not Zack! And he was about to become a Daddy!" said the nurse helplessly.

"Is there anything you can do?" cried Aliza.

"I'm afraid not," said the nurse.

She tried to listen for a heartbeat.

"I'll try anti-venom, but I believe he's long gone," said the nurse sadly.

Suddenly, a boy woke up with a start in a hospital bed next to Zack's.

"Oh, who is he, Nurse? Who is he? Is He Dead? Huh... Huh...IS HE DEAD!?

COOOOOOOOL!" he yelled crazily.

SMACK!

Aliza slapped him in anger.

"OOOH, I Like Them Feisty!!!" yelled the crazy boy.

Aliza was about to knock him senseless what the insane boy just said.

"STOP!" called the nurse.

The nurse quickly pulled out a bottle.

"TAKE YOUR MEDICINE, ARTIMIS!" said the Nurse.

She shoved the bottle in his mouth and made him swallow the liquid.

Suddenly, the boy flopped over unconscious.

"Is he dead?" asked Daniel.

"No, just asleep. I'm sorry Aliza. During a Lemption fight, he was severely beaten in the head by his opponent. He's crazy for right now. Normally, he's very charming," said the nurse, as she injected Zack with a fluid.

They watched Zack for any sign of life.

After several hours nothing had happened.

"I'm afraid…he's gone, Aliza," said the nurse.

Aliza looked from her to Zack and her eyes swelled with tears.

"We'll hold the funeral later," said the Principle kindly.

"Sorry, Aliza. Remember…we're here for you," said Sweetheart, as she gently hugged Aliza's shoulders.

"So are we," said Daniel.

"Th…thanks," stuttered Aliza in tears.

She looked outside and found that it was still raining.

"Funny, isn't it," said Principle Hartford.

"What?" asked Aliza with a weird look.

"Zack's howl causes it to rain. And as soon as he died, it did. He's still with you, Aliza. Eventhough, it may seem impossible. He's bound to turn to crystal any moment now," said Principle Hartford.

"Thank you. But what do you mean turn to crystal?" asked Aliza sadly.

"When Lemptions pass on their bodies crystalize within hours. We don't decompose as humans do when they die. He's going to be as crystal as the one that was given to him on the first day in school," said the Principal, as he starred to the ground.

Aliza nodded with tears in an understanding motion.

Then they all left Aliza to spend her last few hours beside, her husband, Zack.

Chapter 18

A Funeral Secret

Aliza, her friends, her uncle, the Principle, and the whole school attended Zack's funeral.

Zack's parents were wearing black and pouring with tears.

Aliza was also wearing black and kneeled next to Zack's grave.

Most people left after the funeral, except for Sweetheart, Daniel, Shastekae, and Rebecca.

"So Aliza, what are you going to do now that Zack's passed away?" asked Rebecca.

Aliza laid some flowers on Zack's grave.

"I don't know," said Aliza.

As Aliza looked up she noticed a sword like pattern on Shastekae's arm. He was kneeling on the other side of Zack's grave.

"What's that?" asked Aliza.

Shastekae was startled and he quickly pulled down his shirt with a weird frown and stood on his feet.

"Nothing, just a birthmark," he said.

"Nothing or something," said a familiar voice behind them.

It was Uncle Rain.

"Oh. It's you. What do you want?" said Aliza quietly.

"Look, I'm sorry about before and about Zack. Let's start over," said Uncle Rain.

Uncle Rain lifted her up on her feet and gave her a hug.

"You're the only family I have now," said Aliza.

"Hey, what about us!" exclaimed Daniel.

Aliza smiled.

"You to guys," said Aliza.

Then they all had a group hug.

"So what did you mean by what you said about Shastekae's birthmark?" asked Aliza.

"I've been looking for a Lemption with a swordsman Birthmark for a long time," said Uncle Rain.

"Why?" asked Sweetheart.

"He's destined to build a sword for the chosen one to yield." said Uncle Rain proudly.

He slapped Shastekae's back so hard and it almost made him topple over.

"How do I do that? I can't even use a paper clip properly," said Shastekae, as he rubbed his back.

"I'll teach you. Then we'll kill the Vieniem leader and get revenge for Zack." said Uncle Rain.

Aliza smiled at the consideration her Uncle had shown.

"Okay, follow me to the steel area. Where they make the desks," said Uncle Rain.

Then they followed Uncle Rain to the steel area to explain and teach Shastekae how to make the sword for The Chosen One.

Chapter 19

A Sword Developed
2 Weeks Later...

Daniel, Rebecca, Aliza, and Sweetheart walked to the steel production area to see how Shastekae was doing on the sword.

When they walked in and found Shastekae asleep on his metal desk area used for pounding the metal into shape.

His head was sitting on a heated large orange rod that looked as if it was starting to be shaped into a sword.

Daniel realized his position in sleep and woke up Shastekae immediately.

"Huh, huh. What? OUCH MY HEAD!" yelled Shastekae.

He had a burn mark across his forehead.

"THIS IS ALL UNCLE RAIN'S FAULT!!! HE'S BEEN HAVING ME WORK LATE HOURS TO GET THIS STUPID SWORD FINISHED!!!" said Shastekae in anger, while he was hitting the sword with an iron hammer.

Aliza looked on a nearby desk covered with a large sheet of paper and saw a glimpse of the drawn plans of her sword.

SLAM!

Shastekae pounded the desk with his hand and startled Aliza. Then he quickly rolled up the papers, so she couldn't see.

"It's a surprise," said Shastekae with a devilish smile.

"Gees...that's not fair," thought Aliza.

Suddenly, Shastekae looked at his watch and jumped in excitement.

"I AM SO LATE!!!" yelled Shastekae.

He dropped everything and ran to the door

THUD!

Shastekae ran right into the wall, instead of out the door.

"What the...!" said Shastekae under his breath, as he held his head where the burn mark was.

"What's the matter?" asked Aliza.

When Shastekae got up and ran out the door he yelled, "The wedding is today in the main garden! SEE YOU THERE!"

Everyone suddenly looked at their watches.

"Uh oh, we have to get ready!" said Rebecca.

Suddenly, they all ran out the door of the steel production area to their cottages.

Chapter 20

Shastekae's Nightmare

Aliza and the others were all sitting in there seats accompanied by parents, the principle, and Uncle Rain.

Shastekae still wasn't at the front yet.

Suddenly, they heard screaming.

"NO! NOOOOOOO! PLEASE HAVE MERCY! I CHANGE MY MIND! I DON'T WANT TO GET MARRIED! AHHHHHHHHHH!"

They noticed it was Shastekae.

They turned and saw that Shastekae was in the collar and leash again. Sweetheart was in a beautiful gown dragging Shastekae down the aisle.

"You're not running! We're getting married!" said Sweetheart angrily.

"WAIT STOP! NO PLEASE! YOU GAVE ME THE PUPPY EYES! IT'S NOT FAIR! NOOOO!" yelled Shastekae.

They finally made it to the front of the aisle.

An old Lemption with gray hair and ears announced the whole speech, and finally said, "Now do you Sweetheart Lemry take this Lempmale to be your lawful wedded husband."

"I do," said Sweetheart with glowing eyes and a wide smile.

"Now Shastekae Lemry, do you take this wonderful Lempfenine to be your lawful wedded wife," said the old Lemption.

"Can I take a rain check?" said Shastekae, as he layed helpless on the ground.

"LEMRY, SHASTAKAE! HOW COULD YOU?" yelled Sweetheart's mom from the crowd.

"NO PLEASE!" pleaded Shastekae.

Suddenly, Sweetheart bent down and kissed Shastekae with all she had.

Shastekae looked up at Sweetheart with a loving smile.

"I guess…I can learn to love this," said Shastekae.

He got up and pulled out a large Jade heart earring from a white velvet box and pinned it to her left ear.

"I now pronounce these two Lemptions mates for life," announced the old Lemption.

When Shastekae and Sweetheart kissed the leash and collar fell off.

Then everyone cheered in joy.

Suddenly, a deep scary voice filled the sky.

"ALIZA! YOU MAY HAVE EVOLVED, BUT I HAVE YOUR NEED FOR REVENGE! DON'T MAKE ME WAIT! MEET ME AT MY TOWER, IF YOU DARE!"

"It's the Vieniem leader look out!" yelled Aliza.

She some how knew her retched voice.

Aliza, Shastekae, Daniel, Rebecca, and Sweetheart backed together, including Uncle Rain.

"AHHHHH, SHE'S BACK! RUUUUUUUN!" squealed Principle Hartford, like a little girl.

He ran away tripping over his over length robe with his hands in the air.

"WUS!" called Daniel.

"YOU WITCH!" screamed Aliza.

"I KNEW I HAD YOU! YOUR FRIENDS WILL BE NEXT! IF YOU DON'T FIGHT ME!" echoed the Vieniem Leader's voice.

"YOU HAGS MOTHER!" yelled Shastekae.

"QUIET YOU INSOLENT CUB!" echoed the Vieniem Leader's voice.

A powerful wind swirled around them.

"WHEN YOU REACH MY TOWER LOOK FOR KILLAIM! AND DON'T REFUSE! OR YOU'll REGRET IT!" echoed her voice, as it faded out.

They waited, as the wind settled.

"She's gone," gasped Rebecca relieved.

"FINALLY, NOW I WANT ANOTHER KISS FROM YOU SHASTAKAE!" yelled Sweetheart, as Shastekae cringed.

Everybody looked at her stunned considering what had just happened.

"ARE YOU CRAZY? I HAVE TO FINISH THAT SWORD AND DON'T USE THAT LEASH! I'VE HAD IT UP TO HERE WITH YOU!" yelled Shastekae screaming in her face.

Suddenly, Sweetheart's eyes filled with tears and started to cry.

WACK!
WACK!
WACK!

Sweetheart's Mom, Aliza, and Rebecca hit Shastekae on his head.

"OWWW! Okay, I'm sorry, Sweetheart. I've just been really stressed with everything, the school, teaching, the sword, and you know," said Shastekae softly, as he rubbed his head.

Then he kissed her.

Sweetheart then giggled and wiped her eyes.

WACK!

Daniel hit Shastekae on his head.

"WHAT WAS THAT FOR!?" yelled Shastekae, as he rubbed his head.

"Figured I join in," said Daniel.

SMACK!

Rebecca slapped Daniel hard on the back of his head.

"It's over stupid!" exclaimed Rebecca.

"Okay, Honey Buns." said Daniel in a sexy voice.

"I TOLD YOU, NEVER TO CALL ME THAT!" yelled Rebecca.

Rebecca then pushed him into a huge nearby mud puddle and jumped on him beating him mercilessly.

"Uh how about we go to the cabin." said Sweetheart.

"We'll be there in a minute!" called Rebecca, with Daniel's screams of pain from the background.

Sweetheart's Mom congratulated her and Shastekae and left. Then Aliza, Sweetheart, and Shastekae headed to the cottage, finally with Daniel and Rebecca joining them.

Chapter 21

Little Mews for Sweetheart

Once they all reached Sweetheart's and Shastekae's cottage, they all noticed that there was a bunch of math books and papers all over inside.

"Boy, are you obsessed with math," said Daniel with bruises all over him.

"Yeah, well...it's not easy keeping up with five hundred students," said Shastekae.

Shastekae slouched at the kitchen table.

"Mew!"

He jumped up and looked at Sweetheart's cat funny.

"Uh, Sweetheart! How old is your cat?" asked Shastekae.

"Four years," said Sweetheart.

"Then who's is this little fur ball," said Shastekae angered.

"Oh my goodness!" said Sweetheart shocked.

Then they heard a bunch of little mews around the corner of the hall.

Everyone walked over to the next room.

There was Sweetheart's Calico cat and seven little kittens.

Sweetheart had the previous kitten in her hands.

"Awe, they're so cute," said Daniel.

He took off his muddy jacket and layed along the floor next to the kittens.

The kittens immediately take a liking to him and ran over to him. One kitten even ran next to him and curled up to go to sleep.

"Awe... how cute. Don't you think so to, Shastekae? Uuuuh...Shastekae," said Aliza, who was starting to become scared.

Shastekae was cherry red in the face.

"I CAN'T BELIEVE THIS, SWEETHEART! HOW DID THIS HAPPEN!?" screamed Shastekae red with anger.

He was towering over Sweetheart screaming in her face.

Then tears started falling down Sweetheart's cheeks.

"I...I don't know. It could have been an alley cat," she said frightened.

"HOW MANY TIMES! DID I TELL YOU TO GET HER SPAYED!" screamed Shastekae even more.

He picked up a chair and raised it over her head about to throw it across the room.

"NOW I HAVE TO PAY TO FEED EVEN MORE ANIMALS!" yelled Shastekae.

Daniel jumped in the way and got hit by the chair.

"Take the cat and babies and get out! I'll hold him off ," said Daniel quickly.

They all took the cat and her babies and ran out of the cottage.

Once Aliza, Rebecca, and Sweetheart reached a good distance from the cottage and turned around, they began to hear the commotion in the cottage.

"I DON'T NEED TO BE HELD OFF! THAT STUPID CAT HAD KITTENS! I SHOULD BE MAD!" yelled Shastekae at the top of his lungs.

They could hear crashes from inside.

Then they heard Daniel say, "It's better then having cubs."

Then there was silence.

BOOM!

Daniel flew a good ten feet out the door.

Sweetheart, Aliza, and Rebecca ran up to him and Daniel was unconscious.

Shastekae ran out of the cottage away from them.

"WHERE ARE YOU GOING, YOU JERK!?" yelled Aliza.

"TO WORK ON YOUR STUPID SWORD!" he called back.

Sweetheart started to cry heavily and fell to her knees.

"Why did this have to happen?" cried Sweetheart.

"It's not your fault," coughed Daniel, who just awoke.

He had a black and blue swollen face.

"Come on, let's go and take the cat and her babies to my and Zack's cottage," said Aliza, as she turned bitter towards Shastekae.

"But he's dead! How could it be his cottage too?" said Daniel.

"I KNOW THAT YOU IDIOT!" yelled Aliza.

WACK!

Aliza turned and punched Daniel in the face, before Rebecca could even smack him once.

"AHHHHHHHHHHH!" screamed Daniel.

He held his face rolling on the ground screaming in pain.

Aliza turned angrier than ever.

"Come on let's go," said Aliza.

Rebecca bent down to try and help Daniel.

"LEAVE HIM BE!" yelled Aliza with glowing eyes.

Rebecca was startled.

Then they all headed down to her cottage.

Chapter 22

An Unpleasant Visit

Shastekae pounded on the sword and was sweating immensely from the heat.

"You know…you wouldn't have to worry about kittens if you lived with us, we have lions," said a voice behind him.

Shastekae swelled with fear because he knew the voice from the echoes during his wedding.

He turned violently, but saw nothing.

Then he raised the burning steel rod in his gloved hand above his head.

"Come out and show yourself, Witch!" yelled Shastekae.

Suddenly, he felt a sharp pain in his neck.

"AHHHHHHH!" screamed Shastekae.

He felt as though someone had bit his neck.

Suddenly, the steel rod was snatched from his grasp.

He turned and saw The Vieniem Leader's true form.

She was over seven feet tall with jet black bat-like wings with spikes on the bony top and a long wipe-like tail. He saw black markings on her pale green skin, which were the same shapes as his fur patterns. She had the rod in one hand and a long black whip in the other. She was wearing net-like gloves and stockings that covered her arms and legs. Her ears were pointed and her unruly hair was silver with a red band that matched her small red dress.

She looked him up and down in disgust.

"You bit me," yelled Shastekae.

"SHUT YOUR MOUTH! Yuck…You look just like our father," said the Vieniem Leader disgusted and turned away.

Shastekae was confused and then angered.

"What! How would you know about MY father?" asked Shastekae.

He spit on the ground near her black heeled shoes.

"You're so disgusting, brother," said the Vieniem Leader.

"What do you mean BROTHER, Witch!?" asked Shastekae spooked at the thought.

"How could I be related to this Hater of Lemptions?" thought Shastekae

"Stop Calling Me A Witch! My name is Killaim. Your older sister," said, Killaim, the Vieniem leader.

"What do you mean? I couldn't be…your brother," said Shastekae in disbelief.

He looked from her to his sledge hammer.

Then he started to swing at her wildly.

"You're not my sister, You Witch! You're Lying! You're Lying!" yelled Shastekae, as he swung like a mad person.

WACK!

Killaim hit Shastekae with the hot steel rod in his face.

"Shut Up and Listen, brother," she said.

Shastekae fell flat on his butt holding his face moaning in pain.

She started to explain.

"Some years ago the Vieniem Leader, our wonderful mother, secretly mated with a Lemption her age and fell in love. Then THEY bore me and then you… Our mother became hungry for power and killed Lemptions that did not bow to her. So just like the generations before her, she sought to exterminate your wretched kind. But once our father got a sniff of her plan he took her away from the tower and killed her, and, on the same night she lost the scroll and Rein stone Crystal to a group of Lemptions, of which, we are still trying to recover. When our mother was dead he took you to hide in the human world and left me for dead. Then when you were three years old our father was found by the Vieniem clan and was killed. Then left you to live out your puny life on human streets," finished Killaim.

Shastekae was still holding his face, which was now bleeding.

"I'm going to pretend I didn't hear that fake story of yours," said Shastekae.

"Whether you think it is the truth or not, you are going to make me a sword," said Killaim.

"I am not going to make you a sword," said Shastekae bravely.

CRACK!!!

Killaim snapped her whip right in front of Shastekae's feet.

"Now stop being so defiant," said Killaim.

"Why should I make you a sword after you killed, Zack!" yelled Shastekae angrily.

"Well...there is this beautiful Lemption I've heard a lot about...it would be a shame if that girl was to die...and if she was your mate," said Killaim with an evil smile.

"You wouldn't!!!" growled Shastekae.

"Try me!" said Killaim with an evil smirk.

The Vieniem leader grabbed and bit into an apple that was laying on a plate near Shastekae and the apple dried up.

"If you don't start listening...this apple will be your mate's neck," said Killaim evilly.

She threw the dried up apple in Shastekae's lap.

"So you will make me the sword?" she continued firmly.

"No he won't," called a familiar voice.

It was Uncle Rain.

"You'd better get out of here before I kill you," said Uncle Rain.

"Ha, Killaim! You can't even keep up with Shastekae let alone me. While you were ranting on and on I grabbed your whip and rod while you weren't paying attention," he continued.

"Shastekae, you will pay for this!" Killaim called out, as she left with a menacing laugh.

"You're crazy, Uncle Rain!" said Shastekae, who was still holding his bleeding face.

"Don't worry! I requested the help of six very good fighters and Protectors. Their name is the Secret Scout Six." said Uncle Rain Proudly.

At that, they left to Aliza's cottage immediately.

Chapter 23

Meet the Secret Scouts Six

Shastekae ran through the door of Aliza's cottage.

Shastekae's face was still bleeding with a burn and open wound streak across the left side of his face, from his eye down passed his mouth. His face was swollen and his shirt was soaked in blood.

"Oh, My Gosh! What happened to you?" exclaimed Rebecca.

Everyone turned.

Sweetheart was still crying immensely and didn't care to turn.

Shastekae ran down beside Sweetheart and wrapped her in his arms with all his might.

"I'M SO, SO SORRY!" he admitted, "I DON'T KNOW WHAT CAME OVER ME! I'M SO GLAD YOU'RE ALRIGHT!"

Sweetheart pushed him away.

"Let me get some bandages," said Aliza, as she went to the bathroom closet.

Shastekae was mortified that Sweetheart pushed him away.

Aliza quickly wrapped some antiseptic soaked bandages around the side of his face to stop the bleeding.

"Sweetheart, I'm…I'm sorry," said Shastekae.

He tried to give her another hug, but she pushed him away, again.

"Sweetheart! I….I…I'm sorry! I got upset!" said Shastekae.

Suddenly, a kitten came up to Shastekae and pawed him on the leg.

Shastekae picked the kitten up and smiled.

"Look who wants you to smile," said Shastekae in a goofy voice.

Sweetheart still didn't look at him.

Shastekae got annoyed.

"Look I Said I Was Sorry!" said Shastekae in a loud voice.

Sweetheart screamed and ran outside into the dark of night.

"NO SWEETHEART! IT'S NOT SAFE!" yelled Shastekae.

Shastekae couldn't figure out why he was having all these sudden feeling of aggression.

He ran after her quickly and everyone followed.

"Why isn't she safe!?" asked Aliza loudly.

They chased after Sweetheart into the garden park.

"The Vieniem Leader, Killaim, will kill her, if I don't make her a sword, too," said Shastekae scared for his Sweetheart's life.

Finally, they reached Sweetheart at a large fountain.

They couldn't see Sweetheart fully in the darkness.

Suddenly, they heard a wicked laugh in the air.

Once they got closer, they realized the Vieniem Leader had Sweetheart in her clutches.

She had her sharp nails wrapped around Sweetheart's neck.

Aliza's stomach lurched because she remembered the same thing happened to another Lemption girl at Lempschool.

"Let her go, Killiam! I'll make you the sword!" yelled Shastekae.

Killaim laughed.

"To late brother. You had your chance. Now watch your woman die in my hands," laughed Killaim.

Killaim started to fly into the air, but then Aliza transformed and tried to fly. Aliza then realized she had not yet learned how to and felt helpless.

"Oh, can't fly. It's a shame you haven't practiced. Now you can't help your friend," laughed Killaim.

"Let her go!" yelled Aliza.

Shastekae transformed and jumped as high as he could to reach Sweetheart.

Killaim kicked him in the face and Shastekae fell down face first in the ground and detransformed.

Suddenly, chains flew out from the bushes and snagged on to Killaim's wings and she fell to the ground.

Then Aliza pulled Sweetheart from her grasp at the last moment.

Suddenly, six figures jumped in from the shadowed bushes and Uncle Rain was the one who was holding onto the chains.

Killaim broke free and flew off yelling, "I'll have that sword brother!"

Sweetheart leaped into Shastekae's arms.

"You tried to save me. I was so scared," said Sweetheart in tears of fear.

"What did she mean by brother?" asked Aliza.

"Because he's the son of the previous queen or should I say Leader of the Vieniems." said a voice.

"What!" exclaimed everyone.

"Who said That?" called Daniel.

Then the six figures came into view.

"These are the Secret Scout Six." said Uncle Rain, as he wrapped the large chains around his shoulder.

A beautiful twenty-three year old Lemption girl with long purple hair and tail, blue eyes, and dark black ears came up. She had a blue out fit on with dark silver knot-like rags over it and had one knot on her leg, ankle, and arm. She, also, had on purplish-black earrings and necklace and a black and silver striped circle metal attached to the knot by her waist.

"It was me who said that and hi, my name is Naomi," she said.

Daniel was drooling about how gorgeous she looked.

WACK!

Rebecca slapped him.

"Close your mouth and show some manners, Daniel," said Rebecca annoyed.

"Fine," said Daniel.

Daniel turned and walked up to Naomi.

"Forgive me, cutie. Mind if I ask, can I be your mate?" asked Daniel with a smile.

Rebbecca's jaw dropped in unspeakable anger.

Naomi smiled.

Then she drew out her sharp claws and pointed them dangerously close to Daniel's neck.

"I hate guys who are disloyal to their chosen mates," said Naomi.

She slowly pulled back her arm ready to jab him in the throat.

"Okay! Okay! I'm sorry, Rebecca! I love you with all my heart!" said Daniel.

He crawled to Rebecca and bent on one knee.

"Will you marry me?" said Daniel, who was scared out of his wits.

"Your pathetic." said Rebecca.

Then another beautiful twenty-three year old Lemption girl walked up. She had short brown hair, green eyes, and blue ears and tail with a bell attached to it. She had on a purple dress-like shirt with a pink bow on the back and a pink pair of pants.

"Hi. My name is Taomi. Check out my bell," she said.

There was a bell tied to the end of her tail and threw her butt up in the air wiggling her tail to ring the bell.

Daniel leaned over to Shastekae.

"Check out the bell," whispered Daniel.

"Yeah," chuckled Shastekae.

WACK! WACK!

Rebecca slapped them both on their heads.

"I heard that," said Rebecca.

Then another beautiful nineteen tear old Lemption girl came up. She had green hair, eyes, and ears. She had on a very short green skirt and white sleeve puffed shirt. She was holding an orb with light glowing from it.

"My name is Gabriella," she said, "And this is Zebria and Tigerisa. They are sisters, just like Naomi and Taomi."

Zebria was twenty years old and had long black and white striped hair, blue eyes, and one black ear and one white. She was wearing a black and white outfit with fish net sleeves and stockings.

ZEBRIA

Tigerisa was twenty two years old and had orange hair in two pony tails, an orange furry tail, and orange eyes, with tiger patterned ears and outfit. She had a black birthmarks on both sides of her cheeks.

TIGERISA

"And this is Kim," said Tigerisa.

Kim walked up shyly from the shadows. She was extremely cute and had black hair, dark brown ears, and pink eyes. She was wearing a pink buttoned coat-like dress and locket necklace.

KIM

"Kim" jpg file goes here (name "Kim" just below illustration; use Algerian font)

They all introduced each other and headed back to Aliza's cottage.

Chapter 24

Aliza Learns To Fly
Next day...

Uncle Rain was with Aliza in the park.

"Now Aliza...the Vieniem Leader probably learned to fly at a young age. Now it's your turn," said Uncle Rain.

"Alright!" said Aliza.

Aliza transformed and spread her wings. Then she flapped them with all her strength and her feet left the ground.

Aliza was a little shaken by the feel of her weightlessness.

"Okay! Now try to go a little higher," said Uncle Rain.

Aliza flapped her wings even harder.

Then she left the ground even further and she was now almost twenty feet off the ground.

Suddenly, Shastekae ran up with a huge brown paper package.

"ALIZA! ALIZA! I'VE FINISHED YOUR SWORD!" shouted Shastekae.

"SHUT UP! I'M CONCENTRATING!" yelled Aliza in anger.

Shastekae was mortified by her answer.

"UH, UNCLE RAIN...DID I MENTION I'M AFRIAD OF HIEGHTS!" called Aliza.

"SUCK IT UP!" called Shastekae.

Uncle Rain gave him a mean look and Shastekae suddenly became quiet.

"DON'T WORRY, DARLING! YOU'VE GOT IT!" Uncle Rain yelled back.

"HOW DO I MOVE FROM SIDE TO SIDE?" called Aliza.

"TURN YOUR BODY SLIGHTLY AND WING TO YOUR RIGHT TO GO LEFT AND YOUR LEFT TO GO RIGHT!" shouted Uncle Rain.

Aliza turned her body with force and winged to her right, and instead of going to her left she did a twirl in the air and screamed.

Shastekae laughed.

"NICE TRICK, BALLERINA!" called Shastekae.

"DON'T MAKE ME MAD OR I'LL FLY YOU UP HERE AND DROP YOU ON YOUR FAT MELON!" yelled Aliza in anger.

"I JUST WANT TO GIVE YOU THE SWORD!" shouted Shastekae, as he raised the package above his head.

Aliza smiled and then frowned.

"UH, HOW DO I GET DOWN?" called Aliza loudly.

"GLIDE DOWNWARD, THEN TILT YOUR WINGS BACK AND SETTLE ON YOUR FEET!" called Uncle Rain.

"How do you know all this stuff? You don't have wings," asked Shastekae.

"I've seen Vieniems plenty of times in action to know their techniques," said Uncle Rain.

Aliza did exactly what he said and got it right on the dime, except for a little stumble.

"Be careful, Aliza. You can't do that while holding the sword," said Uncle Rain.

Suddenly, Rebecca and Daniel showed up.

"Hi," said Aliza.

"Man, girl. You're huge when transformed. You're bigger than Shastekae's transformation," said Daniel in awe.

"Really, you just noticed," said Rebecca to Daniel.

"OKAY NOW SEE THE SWORD!" yelled Shastekae impatiently.

Aliza smiled.

"Man cool it dude," said Daniel seeing Shastekae's red flushed face.

When Aliza was handed the sword she realized the hefty weight of the packaged sword and set it on the ground.

She ripped off the sword's covering excitedly.

Then she gasped in a smiling expression.

Shastekae was pleased at her response.

The sword had two huge black blades and an interesting gold handle with a familiar stone embedded in its handle.

She picked up the sword.

"What's this stone?" asked Aliza.

"I don't know. Uncle Rain gave it to me," said Shastekae, as he shook his head.

Aliza turned to Uncle Rain.

"You see when you beat me up..." said Uncle Rain.

"YOU BEAT HIM UP! HA, HA, HA, HA, HA!" interrupted Daniel.

"OUCH!"

Rebecca took a bunch of his hair in her fist and ripped at it.

"Uh, well…as I was saying. When that happened…you left the scroll and the Rein stone Crystal, the light crystal I told you about," said Uncle Rain with a smile.

"Oh, COOL!" said Aliza with a smile.

"Ok, I am going to try and fly again," said Aliza.

Aliza flew upward and then suddenly crashed to the ground into a huge mud puddle.

"Nice take off seven four one dumb....not cleared for take off...Oh no, it's on fire!" said Shastekae and made a crashing sound at the end with his voice.

WACK!

Aliza slapped Shastekae and covered his face in mud.

"Wow, you look dumb," said Daniel out of the blue.

WACK!

Rebecca hit Daniel so hard; he hit the ground and was knocked out.

"I need a rinse. My feathers are bunched with mud. By the way, where is everyone else," asked Aliza, as she squeezed chunks of mud and water from her wings.

"Ummm...the...they...they're at your cottage," said Rebecca with a smile.

"Why are they at my cottage? Did I leave the door open?" asked Aliza frowning.

SPLASH!

Uncle Rain was holding a hose and was spraying Aliza with water.

"**AHHHHHHH!**
THAT'S COOOOOOOOOOOLLLLD! IT'S THE MIDDLE OF FALL YOU IDIOT!" screamed Aliza furiously.

Uncle Rain stopped spraying water, after all the mud was gone.

Aliza detransformed in soaked clothes.

"I brought this incase you would need it," said Uncle Rain, as he pulled out a sage colored blanket from his back pack and wrapped it around her.

Aliza found that the blanket was warm and feathery soft.

"It's a thermal blanket and heats up by itself....it was your mothers," said Uncle Rain, as he gave her a hug.

"Thank you, Uncle," said Aliza.

"Okay...now let's get you to your party," said Daniel, as he picked himself slowly off the ground.

"OUCH! AHHHHHH!"

Rebecca soccer kicked him in the head.

"THAT HURT WOMAN!" screamed Daniel.

"She's not supposed to know," said Rebecca.

"What party?" asked Aliza.

They all smiled.

Daniel just held his head in pain.

"Let's go to her cottage," chuckled Uncle Rain.

Then they all headed down the stone path.

Chapter 25

Celebrate!

It was evening and the sun was reaching its end.

Aliza, Uncle Rain, Daniel, Rebecca, and Shastekae reached Aliza's cottage.

When Aliza got in her cottage, it was pitch black and the curtains were closed.

Suddenly, Aliza heard giggles from inside.

Then blinding lights flashed before her eyes.

"SURPRISE!"

Everyone was there, Principal Hartford, Zack's parents, Sweetheart, and even the school nurse.

"WHY ARE ALL YOU HERE?" exclaimed Aliza smiling.

"It's your baby shower, sweetie!" said Lisa, Zack's mom, jumping for joy.

Aliza was filled with happiness.

"We all got you gifts, even all the students and teachers of our school," said Sweetheart.

As they took Aliza to her bedroom, she was amazed to find that there were gifts that towered to the ceiling and filled the room to the kitchen.

"I also brought a ton of goodies, including those sugar cookies you loved so much," said Lisa.

Aliza saw a long table to the side full of food and sweets.

"Oh, guys. This is so great," said Aliza, as her eyes filled with tears.

Lisa and everyone gave Aliza a big hug.

"We knew what to get you, because your last ultrasound showed who your having," said the nurse.

Aliza swelled with tears.

"What are they?" asked Aliza eagerly to know the answer.

The nurse looked at everyone excitedly.

"A BOY AND A GIRL!" she screamed.

Aliza was in disbelief, she was having ferternal twins.

Then Aliza screamed at the top of lungs, "I'M GOING TO HAVE A LITTLE BOY AND GIRL!!!"

Aliza jumped up and down so happy, that everyone joined her.

"Aliza! Open mine first!" said Rebecca quickly.

Rebecca handed her a ribbon wrapped box.

Aliza opened it to find a little blue and a little pink pajama and two cute little pacifiers.

"I love them," said Aliza.

"Open ours next," said Lisa excitedly.

Aliza was shown a huge box, about ten feet long, five feet tall, and six feet wide.

When Aliza opened it, she was speechless.

It was a twin crib, two sides for both babies. One side was blue and the other was a bright pink with two little music ran toys hanging from the top. Then there were also two little blue and yellow sheeted mattresses with two white fleece blankets covering them.

"OH THANK YOU! THANKYOU! THANK YOU! YOU SHOULDN'T HAVE!" said Aliza looking from one side to the other back and forth.

"We wanted the best for our daughter in law. I made the crib, while your Mom made the beds, sheets, and blankets," said Zack's Dad.

Aliza felt so loved she started to cry.

"I love it," she said.

Lisa gave her a hug.

Then sweetheart gave Aliza a big gift.

"It's from both of us," said Sweetheart.

Aliza opened it to find a huge yellow twin baby stroller.

"It's adorable," said Aliza.

"And I got you two baby scrapbooks," said Daniel.

"Awe...your so sweet," said Aliza.

Daniel handed her the scrapbooks.

"Too bad Zack isn't here he would have loved..." said Daniel.

He stopped talking because of the look on Aliza's face.

Suddenly, Aliza burst into tears, screaming, "My Zack! My Poor Zack!"

"Come here you rotten scoundrel!" said Rebecca furiously, as she pulled Daniel by his ear and out the door.

"No, no! Please Rebecca! I didn't mean it! NOOOOOOO!" screamed Daniel.

BOOM! CRASH! SMASH! THUD!

The cottage shook from the beating and they heard Daniel's screams from outside.

Two hours later...

BOOM! THUD! THUD! SMASH! CRASH!

"When is she going to stop beating him?" asked Lisa to herself.

The group just continued to listen to Daniels screams from outside, while Aliza cried as she opened more gifts.

Three hours later...

BOOM! BOOM! BOOM! CRASH! THUD!

Finally, Rebecca came back into the cottage and all everyone saw outside was Daniel's full black and blue body, which was laying motionless on the ground with a severely bloody nose.

"Is he okay?" asked Lisa.

"He'll live," said Rebecca, as she brushed herself off.

"Relax Aliza, don't cry. It's going to be okay, once we get back at Killaim for what she did to Zack," said Uncle Rain.

He patted her on the back trying to comfort her.

"We'll leave in four weeks, after you've got the hang of flying and learning how to fight with the sword," said Uncle Rain.

After that, Aliza got back to opening presents and having fun.

Chapter 26

Journey Through the Forest of Sorrow

4 Weeks Later...

It was dark as night and the air was cold enough to see your breath.

Aliza was now six months pregnant and showing.

"So Aliza have you thought of names yet," said Naomi.

Naomi was holding a large lantern above her head and was being followed by Shastekae, Kim, Sweetheart, Daniel, Rebecca, Taomi, Zebria, Gabriella, Tigerisa, and Aliza's Uncle Rain. They have been walking for many hours.

They were surrounded by gloomy trees and weird plants.

Aliza thought back to what Zack said about the flowers and a tear fell from her eye.

"Definitely Lily for a girl," said Aliza with a frown.

"And a boy," said Naomi.

"I guess ...Zack jr," sniffed Aliza.

"The hurt still burns, eh," said Naomi.

"Yeah," said Aliza.

"You know my husband died and my little boy ...well....I lost him when he was just three, two years ago," said Naomi sadly.

"What happened?" asked Aliza.

"He wandered off from our camp. And well...Vieniem's lions roam all over these parts and unfortunately..." sniffed Naomi.

She couldn't finish.

Aliza put her arm around her to show that she felt the same way.

Taomi over heard the conversation.

"But you don't have to worry about lions when I'm around," said Taomi cheerfully.

"Why's that?" asked Aliza curiously.

Taomi suddenly let out a howl that echoed for miles.

Suddenly a few minutes later, the bushes around them rustled.

Leopards by groups gathered around Taomi.

"Hi, my babies," said Taomi.

"Her howl attracts leopards. And Zebria's howl attracts Zebras and Tigerisa's howl attracts tigers," explained Naomi.

"What does you howl do, Naomi?" asked Aliza.

"My howl can turn day into night. But there's no need for that now." said Naomi with a smile.

Suddenly, there was a huge image in the shadows.

Aliza froze, when she heard the stomps the stranger made.

Suddenly, a huge transformed male Lemption came out of the shadows with leopard spots all over him.

"You called my darling," said the Lemption, as he took Taomi's hand and kissed it.

"I want you too meet, Aliza. She's The Chosen One," said Taomi.

"Wow...nice to meet you. My name is Leo," he said, as he took Aliza's hand and kissed it.

"If only all men were that polite," sighed Rebecca.

"If only you were better looking," said Daniel quietly.

"You runt!" yelled Rebecca.

Rebecca raised her hand to slap him, but a large paw grabbed her wrist.

She turned and found it was Leo.

"Allow me, miss," said Leo.

Daniel cowered beneath his massive shadow.

"Treat women with respect," said Leo.

BOOM!

Daniel was punched straight into a tree.

"Got it," said Daniel, as he passed out.

The tree fell over.

"I'm not going to carry him," said Rebecca.

"Allow me," said Leo politely.

Leo grabbed his ankle and just flopped Daniel's limp body over his shoulder like a rag doll with no feeling of sympathy.

"So why are you lovely ladies and gentlemen doing in this neck of the woods?" asked Leo.

"Honey, you might not like this idea...but we're going to the Vieniem tower," said Taomi.

"WHAT! WHY!" thundered Leo.

"WE HAVE TO HELP ALIZA FIGHT THE VENIEM LEADER! SO DON'T GROWL AT ME." yelled Taomi.

"You know I don't like you putting yourself in dangerous situations," said Leo meaningfully.

"We have to, Leo! Aliza's children and her friends could be in danger if we don't. Including, the future of our kind," explained Taomi.

Leo turned his head and looked from Aliza to the rest of the group.

"Fine, but I'm coming with you. Our Leopard children will be okay, if I leave them behind," grunted Leo.

"Okay," said Taomi, as she nodded her head.

"Not to bother this moment, but I'M HUNGRY!" said Shastekae out of no where.

"WELL THEN, GO OUT TO THAT LAKE OVER BEHIND THAT TREE AND GET A FISH!" yelled Taomi annoyed.

Shastekae walked out to the lake, transformed and turned out his claws. Then he thrashed at the water.

After a few minutes, he finally got a fish.

Suddenly, Leopards pounced on Shastekae trying to get the fish from him.

"GET OFF OF ME YOU FURRY MORANS!" yelled Shastekae.

He pushed and pounded on the Leopards heads.

Leo was furious and grabbed Shastekae by the neck.

"Don't you ever call our children morons or hit them. They're hungry! So give me the fish," said Leo angrily.

"No! I got it first. They're your kids so feed them yourself," said Shastekae.

Leo smiled.

"Fine, I will," said Leo.

Leo used his fingers and whistled.

Suddenly, all the leopards came over to Leo, looking for food.

"Here you go kids. Dinner!" said Leo.

Leo then held Shastekae right over the pack of hungry leopards.

"Hey! HEY! WAIT A MINUTE! NOT ME!" yelled Shastekae.

The leopards clawed towards his body below.

"Okay dear, you had your fun," said Taomi.

Leo growled at Shastekae and threw him in the lake.

Then Leo dived into the lake and disappeared, as Shastekae pulled himself onto dry ground.

A few seconds later, Leo came out of the water with almost a hundred fish in his arms and threw them into the pack of leopards. The leopards shredded and ate all the fish almost at once.

Shastekae starred at them in fear thinking that he could have been their dinner fish, if he hadn't been shown mercy from Leo and Taomi.

"I suppose we should make camp," said Uncle Rain.

Naomi nodded.

Then everyone took off there packs, and started building tents, as Uncle Rain got fire wood.

Chapter 27

A Lost Cause

Aliza and everyone were sitting around a campfire in the middle of an ice cold night.

"ACHOOO!"

"Man! Is It Cold Out Here!" said Shastekae, as he wiped his nose.

Sweetheart came up to him with a blanket.

"Here you go, Honey," said Sweetheart.

"Uh, oh," said Uncle Rain, who was rummaging through his backpack.

"What, Uncle?" said Aliza.

"I was so busy packing weapons....uh...I forgot food," said Uncle Rain.

"WHAT! YOU WERE IN CHARGE OF THE FOOD!" yelled Daniel angrily.

"I'm sorry but..." stopped Uncle Rain.

Suddenly, he heard something in the distance.

"I hear something that way," whispered Uncle, as he pointed in the direction to where the sound was coming from.

They all followed him quietly.

"What if it's a Vieniem?" whimpered Daniel.

They got closer to the noise.

"LA! LA! LA! PICKING FLOWERS FOR MY VASE! LA! LA! LA!" they heard a stranger singing.

"Yeah! That's the sound of a real killer, Daniel," mocked Shastekae.

"Shut up, it could have been a killer," whispered Daniel.

"WHO'S THERE!" said the stranger.

Naomi shined the lantern and aimed the light at the shadowed figure.

"It's a Lemption." she said.

He was good looking and had white hair and ears with blue eyes.

"SHOW YOURSELF! DON'T MAKE ME USE DEADLY FORCE!" yelled the stranger.

He held up a squeaky toy mouse.

"THAT'S DEADLY FORCE! HA! HA! HA!" laughed Daniel.

Shastekae started laughing too.

"YOU ASKED FOR IT!" yelled the stranger.

The stranger let out a blood curtailing howl and threw the toy into the open.

Then suddenly the toy grew into a huge armed red eyed robot, as big as a house.

"Who knew," said Shastekae with a weak frightened chuckle.

Daniel let out a deafening girlish scream.

"WE MEAN NO HARM!" yelled Uncle Rain quickly.

He stepped out into the light.

"THEN WHO ARE YOU?" asked the stranger.

"WERE LEMPTIONS JUST LIKE YOU!" called Uncle Rain.

"Well…except for me," thought Uncle Rain.

The stranger let out another howl and the monster robot shrunk back down into a little mouse squeaky toy.

They all came up to meet the stranger.

"Nice Howl! Are you the squeaky toy invader?" laughed Shastekae.

"No, but it's nice to meet you," said the stranger.

He shook Shastekae's hand with a smile on his face.

It made Shastekae annoyed.

"And who are the rest of you lovely folks?" asked the stranger.

"That's none of your business," said Shastekae.

"Oh, pardon me. My name is Alexander. I'm nineteen years old," said the boy.

"How come you never went to our school? And why are you so ugly!" said Shastekae yelling in his face.

"SHASTEKAE!" said Sweetheart, as she pulled Shastekae by the arm back in the group.

"Leave me alone, woman!" exclaimed Shastekae.

"ANSWER THE QUESTION?" yelled Shastekae even more.

Everyone was surprised at Shastekae's temper.

"Glad to. I was raised by traitors of the Vieniem clan." said Alexander calmly.

Everyone gasped.

Then there was silence and all they could hear was the sound of crickets chirping.

"Your SO WRONG!" yelled Daniel at a distance.

"You want meet Mr. Squeaky again," said Alexander.

"No," whimpered Daniel again.

"You mean to say you were raised by Vieniems," said Uncle Rain disbelievingly.

"Yes sir. I have a picture of them at home. Come on! I haven't had company in a long time," said Alexander.

"I don't know," said Uncle Rain suspiciously.

"Come On, Mr. Rain! IT'S FREEZING!" called Daniel shivering from the end of the group.

"I guess we could use the food," said Uncle Rain quietly.

"Are you sure?" whispered Naomi.

"If it is a trick...we'll use full force," said Uncle Rain, as he nodded.

"Don't be too hard on them," said Shastekae with a smile.

They looked at him weird.

Uncle Rain just shook his head at Shastekae.

So they all followed Alexander through the Forest of Sorrow.

Chapter 28

Lost and Found

Once, they came to an opening in the Forest of Sorrow they found a huge mansion in the center of the opening.

Daniel noticed a bunch of squeaky toys sitting around the entire mansion, and screamed, "They're gonna get us RUUUN!"

Then he hid behind Rebecca.

"Don't worry their not gonna get you...yet," said Alexander with a devious smile on his face.

Daniel gave him a scared expression.

"Just kidding," said Alexander, as he shook his head.

"Man what a piece of junk place to live," said Shastekae.

"It's not on the inside though. I just leave it like that so it will not arise suspicion from any of Killaim's passing Vieniems," explained Alexander.

As he opened the large antique door it made a loud creak and they went inside.

Once they were inside, they noticed a spiraling marble staircase that went up a second floor with many rooms. There was a crystal chandelier that glistened with magnitude forty feet from the ground, along with many wooden antique walls leading through wooden floors to many different areas of the mansion.

"Come on, this way. You must be hungry," said Alexander.

They followed Alexander through a hall to the dinning room, with a table long enough to hold thirty people covered with clothed napkins, silver ware, and china plates and cups.

"Sit down. I'll get some food. I have lots of leftovers," said Alexander, as he left to the kitchen.

Aliza and the others sat down on cushioned antique chairs.

"What a huge place to live in," said Aliza in awe.

"Yeah, but I'm still not comfortable about knowing he was raised by Vieniems," said Uncle Rain.

"This could be a trap," said Naomi.

Everyone stayed alert.

"Then why is he so nice," said Aliza, as she sat next to Naomi.

"I don't know," said Uncle Rain.

Alexander came back with a rolling cart full of food.

He set a huge turkey in the center of the table, followed by a huge pot of potatoes and a smaller pot of gravy. Then two pots of corn and peas mixed with carrots.

"Man! Dude, how did you make all this food so quick?" asked Daniel.

"They were all left over's. From when my Auntie and Uncle came to visit. I love to cook," said Alexander.

"Wait a minute. I thought you said you were raised by Vieniems," said Uncle Rain.

"Yeah!" agreed the rest of them.

"They were also traitors of the Vieniem clan. They are coming over for a visit real soon," said Alexander proudly.

"WHAT!" yelled everyone.

"You can't be serious," said Naomi in shock.

"They'd love to meet you guys," said Alexander with a smile.

"OKAY! TIME TO GO!" exclaimed Daniel, while he sat next to Uncle Rain.

He got up and started to walk.

Suddenly, Uncle Rain grabbed him by the collar of his shirt and sat him back down.

"Don't be rude. Now eat up everyone we need our strength!" said Uncle Rain.

"Yeah, don't worry. They won't hurt you. They raised my wife," said Alexander, while he sat next to Uncle Rain at the end of the long dining table.

"Then where is she," asked Naomi, while she sat next to Daniel as well as Aliza.

Alexander looked down with a sad look.

"She was killed by... by lions. While...while looking for food," sniffed Alexander.

"How do we know you're not lying?" exclaimed Uncle Rain, as he got up and threw his fork down from his hand.

Alexander broke into tears and burst out crying.

"My Wife, My Poor Wife!" cried Alexander, as he poured tears.

"SIT DOWN, RAIN!" screamed Naomi.

Naomi ran up to Alexander and held him in her arms.

Alexander kept crying profusely and Uncle Rain sat down starting to feel a little sorry for him.

"Sorry, kid. I had no idea," said Uncle Rain.

Alexander started to settle down and Naomi gave him a napkin.

"It's okay, baby." said Naomi, as she gave him a hug as if he was her own.

"She was the best thing that ever happened to me. And I lost her to Killaim's wicked lions," sniffed Alexander.

"It's alright, same thing happened to my son." said Naomi softly.

"So when are your aunt and uncle coming?" asked Aliza with a shiver down her spine.

"Soon, I suppose." said Alexander.

Naomi went back to her seat.

"So where's your parents?" asked Uncle Rain.

Alexander made a frown.

"They were killed by Killaim's minions, when I was but an infant," said Alexander, as a tear fell from his eye.

Everyone felt sorry for him.

"Sooo...where exactly did you come from?" asked Uncle Rain.

"My parents said they found me on the dead body of a woman Lemption in a cave with a dead fire. And supposedly my father had been bitten and fallen off a cliff," said Alexander with a frown.

"Impossible," said Uncle Rain thinking.

"Uh, Uncle, didn't you say..." started Aliza.

"Shhh..." interrupted Uncle Rain.

He thought.

"Could you provide proof?" asked Uncle Rain.

"Sure. Just a minute," said Alexander, as he left the room.

"Do you think it could have been my...parents?" asked Aliza.

"It may be possible, there weren't Lemption ultrasound machines in your parent's time," said Uncle Rain.

"It can't be," said Aliza disbelievingly and she started to feel overwhelmed.

Alexander came back with two stones, a pink and green one.

"Impossible," said Uncle Rain under his breath.

"That can't be true," thundered Aliza.

"It's true Aliza, these...are your Mom's and Dad's stones." said Uncle Rain shocked.

"Her parent's stones. That means I have...a sister." said Alexander slowly.

"Yep. Aliza. Let alone The Chosen one," said Uncle Rain, as he pointed to her.

"SISTER!" said Alexander, as he ran over to give her a big hug.

Aliza pushed him away, but he pushed back trying to give her a hug.

"I can't be true," said Aliza still overwhelmed.

Uncle Rain nodded.

"It is," he said.

"SISTER, GIVE ME A HUG!" said Alexander.

"Okay!" said Aliza with a weird expression.

Aliza gave Alexander a hug, with a little pat on the back, but Alexander wouldn't let go and practically squeezed her to death.

"Hon, let go. She's pregnant," said Naomi quickly.

"Oh, Sorry," said Alexander.

Alexander let go and Aliza gasped for air.

Suddenly, they heard the front door open.

"WE'RE HERE!" said two voices.

"AUNTIE, UNCLE!" yelled Alexander, as he ran into the next room.

Everyone was horrified at his response.

They heard his voice from the entrance down the hall.

"Guess What! I Have Guests! AND ONE OF THEM IS MY SISTER!" yelled Alexander childishly.

"What!" said a man's voice.

"Well, let's go meet them," said a woman's voice.

Everyone sat stiff as a board because they were extremely uncomfortable with the situation.

As soon as they walked in, Daniel hid under the table and screamed, "HIDE! THEY'LL KILL US!"

Both Vieniems were about ten feet tall and had fangs, long wipe-like tails, pale green skin, pointed ears, and bat-like wings. The woman was beautiful and had red hair and her handsome husband's hair was black.

"Nice to meet you," said the woman, as she held her hand out to Uncle Rain.

Uncle Rain just sat there staring at her.

Uncle Rain took a look at her husband, staring into an awe of no return.

"Is it me?" asked the woman to her husband.

"No, no," he said.

"Sorry, my name is Ashley. And my husband's name is Leonard," said the woman.

"Seems like you folks. Haven't had a good experience with our kind before," said Leonard rubbing his neck in guilt because of his species present history.

"Uhhhhhh...no," said Uncle Rain, still in awe.

Leo suddenly got up from his seat next to his wife, Taomi, and Aliza, and shook Leonard's hand.

"Nice to meet a fellow, Leo," said Leo.

"Leo, Sit Down!" yelled Taomi.

"Sorry Honey," said Leo.

He went back to his seat next to her and sat his huge form gently on the chair, which surprisingly didn't collapse from his weight.

"Sooooo...ummmmm...where...uhh...did you come from?" asked Uncle Rain, as he cleared his throat.

"We were born in the Northern tribes. The ones who betrayed wicked Killaim and her minions." said Leonard with a frown.

"How many of you are left?" asked Aliza.

"Just us...Alexander's parents were killed by Killaim's minions and the others...well...they didn't survive the first attack on the village." said Ashley with a frown.

"My parents died protecting me," said Alexander with sad eyes.

"Where did you get this mansion?" asked Taomi.

"Ashley, me, and his parents built it," said Leonard.

"Wow," said Shastekae.

"Then where were you Alexander, when your parents were killed?" asked Taomi.

"I was wandering stupidly off the protective surroundings and ran into a couple of Killaim's minions. My parents came to my rescue and told me to run, so I did. But they never came back," said Alexander in tears.

"You poor thing," said Naomi.

"We tried to find them, but they were dead by the time we did," said Ashley.

Alexander burst into to tears and started to cry, so Ashley bent down from her tall structure and held him close.

"There was nothing we could do." said Leonard.

"Rain, I think they're telling the truth." said Kim quietly, while she sat next to Taomi.

Alexander suddenly stopped crying once he looked in Kim's direction.

"Maybe. But we must still stay alert. No offense." said Uncle Rain to Ashley and Leonard.

"None taken. We understand." said Leonard.

Suddenly, Alexander walked up to Kim and looked at her intensely.

"What's your name?" asked Alexander.

Kim blushed.

"Kim." she said.

Ashley giggled.

"What's up with him?" asked Uncle Rain.

Then Ashley bent down and whispered in his ear.

"That's the first thing he did when he met, his wife," said Ashley.

"Oh No. Boy, Get Away From Her!" called Uncle Rain to the end of the table.

"Sorry, Mr. Rain," said Alexander, as he slowly backed away from Kim remembering that Kim called him "Rain."

Kim gave Alexander a wink.

"SHE LOVES ME!" screamed Alexander.

"Get A Life!" said Daniel in response to Alexander's actions.

WACK!

Rebecca reached over and snapped Daniel's fingers hard with her fork.

Daniel just rubbed his pain stricken hand after in silence.

All the girls at the table laughed, including Alexander's Uncle and Aunt.

"Boy, I'll Say IT Again. SIT!" yelled Uncle Rain, as he got up from his seat.

Alexander ran back to his seat and sat.

"If he was so important to you, then why didn't you bring him to the school?" said Uncle Rain angrily.

"Because if we showed up with him, we would have been killed," explained Leonard.

Alexander totally ignored the conversation.

"What do you do for fun, Kim?" asked Alexander, while he leaned on his hands.

He was admiring her beautiful face in an awe.

She smiled shyly and said nothing.

"She doesn't fight...ever. And we've never seen her transformation," said Zebria, while she sat next to Kim.

Kim frowned.

"Why not?" asked Alexander.

"It takes a lot to get her mad. Say the wrong thing and she'll get really upset," chuckled Tigerisa, who was sitting next to Gabriella.

"One time she was surrounded by about thirty Vieniems, we weren't even there. By the time we did get there…about two minutes later, all of them were dead," said Gabriella.

"Come here. I want to show you some pictures of Alexander when he was a baby," said Leonard.

Everyone followed Leonard out of the room.

Leonard brought them passed the stair case and across a hall way into a room with the walls covered by frames.

"This is Alexander," said Leonard, as he pointed to a picture.

In the picture there was as a little boy with large blue eyes, cute little white ears, and white long hair in a little blue outfit with a blank expression on his face.

"Yep…Aliza, your father also had blue eyes. And you got your eyes from your mother," said Uncle Rain.

"What did they look like?" asked Aliza.

"Well, sure you saw them in the pictures I gave you," said Uncle Rain with a smile.

"Oh yeah. Well, What did my father look like again?" asked Aliza.

"Well, let's see. He was a tall thin man, but had a lot of strength than you could imagine. And was handsome, like me in those years. And well you get my the picture," said Uncle Rain.

"And who is this?" asked Daniel drooling.

There was a picture of an amazingly beautiful slender girl Lemption, in a beautiful yellow peasant like outfit. She had very light silvery blond hair and pink furry ears and tail with golden eyes. She was sitting in a canoe with light glistening through the trees with her hand in the air like she was waving.

"That was his wife, Ameilia," said Ashley with a frown.

"What a shame," said Zebria.

"Yep, she was the most gorgeous thing to lay eyes on. And after she died...Alexander's never been the same since. In fact, that's why he started calling us Auntie and Uncle. To try and forget his loss," said Leonard.

Uncle Rain looked at the picture shaking his head and then looked to everyone with a frown.

Suddenly, Uncle Rain noticed Alexander and Kim were missing from the group.

"WHERE IS KIM AND ALEXANDER!?" thundered Uncle Rain.

Everyone ran back to the dinning room and found Kim and Alexander were kissing romantically.

Uncle Rain's face grew bright red and screamed, "WHAT ARE YOU TWO DOING? WE HAVE A MISSION TO ACCOMPLISH AND YOU TWO ARE MAKING OUT LIKE YOUR ON A HONEY MOON!"

They continued kissing and completely ignored Uncle Rain's rage.

"Awwwe," said Ashley.

"Looks like he found his new mate," chuckled Leonard.

"OVER MY DEAD BODY!" thundered Uncle Rain.

He started to stomp in their direction and suddenly Naomi pulled him back and shook her head.

"Let me take care of this," said Naomi, as she went next to Kim and Alexander.

Then she split the two of them apart forcefully.

"What are you doing?" asked Naomi horrified at Kim's actions.

"He said he loves me, and said he'd never leave me if I loved him, too. Nobody's ever said that to me before, so truthfully...or at all," said Kim.

" Of course I feel sorry for him but...but, What's wrong with you girl? He was raised by Vieniems," said Naomi.

"And that means..." said Kim with a frown.

Alexander looked at Kim lovingly.

"THAT YOU'RE STUPID!" yelled Naomi.

WACK!

Everyone gasped.

Kim slapped Naomi, so hard it left a red mark on her face.

"IS THAT A CHALLENGE!" screamed Naomi.

"Yes." said Kim firmly.

Chapter 29

Kim's Challenge

Everyone was outside in a dark gloomy opening in the backyard of Alexander's mansion.

Kim and Naomi were on opposite sides of the opening, while everyone else was on the stone porch right outside the backdoors.

"No way! Is Kim going to beat our leader!?" asked Tigerisa stunned.

"My sister's the strongest Lemption ever...Kim won't stand a chance," said Taomi, who was looking scared.

"Well...as far as I know. Naomi's never lost a battle with Vieniems," said Uncle Rain.

"With Kim it's no different, Naomi is still going to win," said Zebria.

"Even when she was little, Naomi could still beat up the biggest, baddest grown up Lemption in our village," said Taomi.

"Well, does Kim have an advantage?" asked Aliza.

"No, we still don't even know what her howl does," said Gabriella.

Uncle Rain turned out his wallet and whispered to Leo, "Do you want to place a bet? I'll put in a hundred dollars on Naomi."

"Sure. I'll put in fifty," said Leo, as pulled out a wad of money from a worn out cloth pouch around his waist and set it on the ground next to Uncle Rain.

Then a distance away, Daniel noticed Shastekae walk away from the backyard into the dark gloomy Forest of Sorrow.

Daniel walked up to Shastekae and asked, "Where are you goin' dude?"

Suddenly, Shastekae turned with a mysterious mark across the side of his face, where Killaim had hit him with the burning steel rod.

Suddenly, Shastekae grabbed Daniel by the collar of his shirt and lifted him off his feet.

"None of your business," whispered Shastekae, as the black mark began to glow.

Then Shastekae dropped Daniel back on his feet and started to walk into the Forest of Sorrow again.

Daniel shrugged his shoulders and walked back to the group silent and curious at all of Shastekae's recent actions.

Then Daniel and Alexander noticed the wads of money being thrown to the ground and saw there was a bet being made and began to walk over.

Once they got there, they looked at each other with a weird smile.

"If you're going to bet. Someone needs to bet on the other person," said Alexander.

"Well...we both know who's going to win," chuckled Uncle Rain.

"I'm in! I'll take an 'I owe you' for two hundred on Kim," said Daniel.

"You're crazy boy!" whispered Uncle Rain with a chuckle.

Leo and Uncle Rain laughed quietly.

"And I'll bet all this on my darling, Kim," said Alexander.

Alexander threw a whole bag of gold coins, four star Sapphires and four star Rubies on the pile.

"Boy, Are you nuts! Do You Realize How Much Money That Is!?" yelled Uncle Rain quietly.

"Anything for my Kim, besides I have a whole pile of this stuff in my basement," said Alexander.

"From where?" asked Uncle Rain suddenly.

"Oh, a lot of riches were found underneath where my family dug and buit our mansion," explained Alexander with a smile.

Uncle Rain, Leo, and Daniel looked at each other in awe.

"All right boy. If she wins this challenge you can date her and have her as your wife, if you both choose to later. But you're asking for a painful lesson," said Uncle Rain with an evil smirk.

Alexander nodded in agreement.

Then Uncle Rain walked into the center of the opening.

"First one down for five minutes loses!" echoed Uncle Rain.

Uncle Rain moved back to the stone porch, while Naomi prepared herself and transformed.

She's had all black fur except for a long purple main going down her back and across her tail. Her wolf like jaw had teeth the size of a human finger and her body was as tall as eight feet high and her furry shoulders were as wide as four feet.

When she stood on her hind legs they were long, and her back paws were huge, even when she stood up from the toes. Her claws on her paws were long, sharp, and deathly white.

Kim just stood in her position silent with an angry expression staring on into Naomi's eyes.

"GO!" yelled Uncle Rain.

Suddenly, Naomi dug her claws into the dirt and leaped for Kim.

Kim just stood still.

As soon as, Naomi latched back onto the ground, Kim had no time to act.

Naomi punched Kim with full force.

Kim flew dead center into a tree ten feet away and fell to the ground.

She layed there motionless.

"OH NO!" yelled Alexander, as he ran to her aid, but then Uncle Rain pulled him back.

"One minute!" called Uncle Rain.

Naomi looked at her pitiful body.

"Humph, that was easy," huffed Naomi, as she shrugged her shoulders and detransformed and started to walk back to the group.

"Two minutes!" yelled Uncle Rain.

Everyone turned away from the scene.

"Three minutes!" called Uncle Rain.

THUD!

A rock hit Naomi's head.

Everyone gasped.

Kim was standing up and holding her arm.

"You're not done with me yet," chuckled Kim, as wiped her bloody nose on her sleeve.

"YOU STILL DON'T GIVE UP, FOR YOUR VIENIEM LOVER! DO YOU!" called Naomi.

Kim looked at her with a serious face and smiled.

Suddenly, Kim let blood curtailing howl and she was gone.

Naomi retransformed using her ears to listen for any sound of Kim.

"Humph, her howl turns her invisible," said Naomi to herself.

"Not quite," said Kim's voice behind her.

Naomi quickly turned around and whipped her claws at the air.

Naomi saw nothing and heard nothing.

"But real close," said Kim's voice next to her ear.

Naomi whipped her claws next to her and ended up clawing herself in the face.

"WHERE ARE YOU, KIM?" yelled Naomi, as she held her bleeding face with one eye open.

Suddenly, leaves flew from the ground and formed a smiley face in the air.

"Right Here," echoed Kim's voice in Naomi's ears.

Naomi suddenly became frightened.

She whipped her other claw at the leaves and they just fell back to the ground.

"Freaky," said Daniel.

"Shhhh..." said Uncle Rain, as he watched intently.

Naomi started to walk in circles looking for Kim.

"What are you looking for? I'm right here," echoed Kim's voice again in Naomi's ears.

Naomi started to become frantic and began looking through the leaves to find Kim.

"Now...It's MY TURN," echoed Kim's Voice in the air.

Suddenly, clouds of dirt and leaves flew into the air and the wind circulated and formed a cloudy statue of Kim. She was almost fifty feet tall and had her clouded hand in the air.

Suddenly, her arm turned around and around and formed a funnel cloud in the sky.

"DANG!" said Daniel in awe.

Naomi trembled in fear at the sight of what Kim was creating.

"Are You Nuts, Kim? You'll Kill All Of Us!" screamed Naomi.

"NO, JUST YOU!" echoed Kim's threat even louder.

"Uh oh," said Naomi.

So she started to run away, but suddenly the wind pulled her back.

"She can control the wind," said Uncle Rain in awe.

"No, I Also Become Part Of The Wind and control it," echoed Kim.

"NO STOP!" cried Naomi.

"TOO LATE!" said Kim.

Suddenly, the funnel cloud Kim created became a tornado, but surprisingly none of the wind was hitting the mansion, the surrounding trees, or the group. Only Naomi was in danger. Kim was in complete control of the wind.

Naomi was sucked into the funnel and was whiplashed around in circles. Then rocks were picked up by the wind and swirled in the tornado. The rocks began to pummel her almost to death.

Finally, the wind died down and Kim's form disappeared.

Then Naomi fell forty feet and hit into a rock below her and cracked it.

Then another blood curtailing howl was released in the air and Kim appeared where she originally stood, still holding her arm in pain.

"Is she really dead?" asked Taomi fearfully.

"No, I just taught her a lesson in love," said Kim with an evil smirk.

Everyone stood in amazement.

Naomi just laid on the cracked rock unconscious.

Uncle Rain then raised his arm in awe and starred at his watch.

"One Minute!" he called.

Everyone stood in silence.

"Two Minutes!" he called again.

Kim stared at Naomi's body in anger.

"Three Minutes!" called Uncle Rain again.

Then Naomi's body started to move.

"Four Minutes!" called Uncle Rain once more.

Then a miracle happened.

Naomi pulled herself to her feet.

"Is that all you got? I'm not through yet!" chuckled Naomi, as she wobbled on her feet.

Kim calmly walked slowly up to Naomi.

"Oh really..." said Kim with an evil grin.

BOOM!

Kim punched Naomi ten yards into a tree and the tree was obliterated into mulch.

Naomi detransformed and her body layed on the chips and leaves of the tree.

Then five minutes had passed.

Then Uncle Rain angrily grunted loudly, "TIME! KIM WINS!"

Everyone cheered.

"She's amazing," said Tigerisa.

"Who knew," said Taomi.

"WOW! EVEN SHE COULD BEAT ME UP! AND WITHOUT EVEN TRANSFORMING," exclaimed Leo, as he clapped his large paws together.

"She's definitely a tough girl," chuckled Leonard, as his whip-like tail swung proudly.

"She's perfect for our little Alexander," said Ashley.

Kim then walked up to Alexander, as Uncle Rain watched in horror.

"Here's my prize," said Kim.

She kissed him for almost ten minutes and then wrapped their arms around one another.

Uncle Rain's face then grew bright red in anger and went back inside the mansion slamming the door behind him.

"AHHHHHHHHHHHHHHHH!"

They all heard him scream furiously inside the mansion.

"So we win the money," said Daniel, as his face lit up in joy.

"I don't want it. You can keep it," said Alexander, as he continued kissing Kim.

Daniel looked at the money below his feet.

THUD!

Daniel passed out on the pile of money.

"My idiot," said Rebecca under her breath, as she shook her head in embaressment.

She just continued to shake her head.

Uncle Rain came out of the mansion, still angered.

Suddenly, they heard hissing in the direction of the cracked rock that broke Naomi's fall.

"What's that sound coming from?" asked Aliza.

"Oh no," said Uncle Rain.

Daniel became contious a few seconds before the hissing started.

"I think it's coming from under the rock. I'll go check it out," said Daniel, as he started off in that direction.

Uncle Rain grabbed him by the collar of his shirt and threw him back into the group.

"Don't go out there!" whispered Uncle Rain.

"What's the matter?" asked Aliza loudly.

"Shhhhhhhhhhh...it's a Sniper," said Uncle Rain quietly.

"What's a Sniper?" asked Tigerisa.

"It's a deadly poisonous lizard. You don't even need to feel a thing to know it bit you," said Uncle Rain.

They watched the cracked rock silently and then a huge six foot black lizard with a long tail one and a half times it's body length crawled out of a hole under the cracked rock.

The lizard sniffed the air and the rock, and then crept silently to Naomi's body.

"OH NO, YOU DON'T!" said Uncle Rain.

Uncle Rain reached into his pack and pulled out a chain with a sickle connected to the end.

Then lizard swished its long tail like a wipe and made a loud crake in the air.

"Yep, he's mad!" said Ashley.

"How do you know?" asked Aliza.

"When a sniper is mad, it sends a warning with its tail," whispered Uncle Rain.

"What are we going to do?" said Daniel loudly.

"Shhhhhh! You Idiot!" hushed Rebecca.

"To late," said Uncle Rain.

The lizard suddenly changed directions, do to Daniel's loud mouth.

"Stand Back!" said Uncle Rain.

Uncle Rain raised the sickle above his head a started to swing the chain, as the lizard slithered to them.

Suddenly, the lizard picked up speed running in to take a bite out of anyone closest to it.

"It's moving to fast I can't target it. RUN INTO THE MANSION!" yelled Uncle Rain.

Everyone pulled open the doors with all their might, but the lizard was already to close.

Sweetheart was the closest in the Sniper's path.

Suddenly, a dark image shot out of the nearby trees and latched onto the lizard with it's claws, and sunk its teeth into the Snipers neck.

The lizard struggled and rolled over to release the creature's grasp.

The Sniper, suddenly, stopped moving and flopped dead to the ground.

Then the Creature got up a walked into the light.

It was Shastekae, with the sniper's blood dripping from his jaw.

Shastekae wiped the blood from his jaw with his furry arm and detransformed.

"Shastekae you're a life saver!" exclaimed Sweetheart, as she threw her arms around him.

Shastekae then pulled her off of him.

"Whatever," said Shastekae firmly.

"Enough fun for tonight. Why don't we all get some rest," said Uncle Rain, still with a frown.

"You're all welcome to spend the night in all twelve of our guest bedrooms," said Alexander with a smile.

"Finally, I get to sleep alone!" exclaimed Rebecca.

"Yeah, and I don't have to listen to you snore," said Daniel.

WACK!

Rebecca kicked Daniel where the sun doesn't shine.

THUD!

Daniel fell to his knees in pain unable to make a sound.

Everyone was separated from girls and boys, except for Taomi and Leo.

Then they all went inside for a good night rest, as Uncle Rain carried Naomi's body up the stairs.

Chapter 30

The Terror of Death

Aliza is running through the Forest of Sorrow, away from Alexander's mansion. She looks behind her seeing a dark figure chasing after her. "I'll get you and your followers!" echoed a familiar male's voice. She couldn't match the voice. Then she heard a cry beyond the forest in front of her. She found it familiar just as the first voice she heard. "HELP! PLEASE, HELP ME!" yelled the second voice. As the voice pleaded in screams, she noticed it was a girl's cry. "PLEASE, HELP! HELP!" screamed the girl even louder. Aliza looked behind her and the dark figure was gone and flew over her. She still ran, then suddenly, the different man's voice echoed in the distance, "Help Your Friend!" Suddenly, Aliza tripped over something and when she saw what she tripped over her heart stopped. She looked next to her to find a dead girl's body covered in blood. Aliza was horrified and scrambled away from the dead girl's body. She couldn't recognize the girl's face because of how dark it was in the surrounding trees. Suddenly, the moonlight emitted through the trees to reveal the dead girl was Zebria with her lifeless expression staring straight into the sky. Then something flew above her, so she looked above the trees and saw the dark figure flying with batwings and red eyes that was chasing before. However, she couldn't see the face of the stranger, but noticed he had Lemption ears and tail. "HA! HA! HA! I KILLED HER!" he said with a maniacal laugh. Howvever, Aliza didn't understand because the man's voice nearest to the dead girl, Zebria, was different then this voice. Suddenly, he pulled out a sword and said evilly, "Your brother is next!" Then suddenly the man toke the sword and slashed before her eyes, slicing at her legs.

"AHHHHHHHHHHHHH!"

Aliza screamed.

She awoke and covered in sweat and shaking in her brother's dark guest room.

Suddenly, her door was opened and Uncle Rain came in.

"What's the matter?" he asked, as he switched on the lights.

"My...Brother's Next!" said Aliza still shaking.

"Who was first?" asked Uncle Rain.

Suddenly, the whole group including Alexander and his Uncle and Aunt came into the room. Also Naomi came in on wobbly legs, black eyes, and bruises all over her body; surprisingly with no broken bones.

"What was the screaming for?" asked Daniel with a yawn, as he rubbed his eyes.

"Zebria!" said Aliza suddenly.

"Just a nightmare," said Uncle Rain.

"HELP! AHHHHHHHHHHHH!"

There was a scream outside the mansion.

Everyone, including Uncle Rain and Aliza, came outside the front door.

It was Zebria.

Half her body was crystallized from the waist to her feet.

The rest of her body was cut up and bleeding.

She was half dead.

Tigerisa pushed through the group.

"ZEBRIA! ZEBRIA! SISTER, PLEASE TELL US WHAT HAPPENED!" cried Tigerisa, as her eyes filled with tears.

"The Terror of Death...sha...sha...ste..." said Zebria slowly in her dying breath.

"WAIT SISTER WE...WE CAN'T...DON'T DIE! WE CAN STILL SAVE YOU!" screamed Tigerisa, as she shook her head with tears rivering down her face.

Tigerisa watched helplessly, as Zebria closed her eyes and her head fell to the side life less.

"SISTER! SISTER WAKE UP!" said Tigerisa shaking her sister's shoulders.

Then she turned to Naomi and Uncle Rain.

"SAVE HER! HELP!" screamed Tigerisa.

Naomi kneeled and checked her pulse.

Then Naomi turned to Tigerisa.

"She's gone," said Naomi, as a tear fell from her eye.

"How Could This Be?" asked Uncle Rain angrily.

"I just had a nightmare of Zebria's death," said Aliza sadly.

"You did?" asked Rebecca sadly.

"Yeah, But I didn't see who the killer was," said Aliza in tears.

Then suddenly Zebria's whole body crystallized before their eyes.

Everyone was struck by what they saw.

"Who could have done this?" asked Naomi sadly.

"Well, I know that only a sword forged by Lemption crystals could have caused her crystallization so fast, when she was cut by that sword," said Uncle Rain thinking.

"Who do you suppose who could have done this?" asked Tigerisa with tears pouring from her eyes.

"And who's the terror of death?" asked Rebecca.

"Well, after the legend of the Chosen One, they say that one of her followers will turn to the Vieniems side after bitten from the Vieniem Leader herself," said Uncle Rain still thinking.

"Who could have been bitten?" asked Gabriella.

Rebecca turned to Daniel with a fowl frown.

"WHAT! IT WASN'T ME!" said Daniel offended.

"Well, Who Else Is Stupid enough to be bitten," said Rebecca.

"No, she wasn't trying to pronounce Daniel," said Tigerisa.

"Then who?" asked Rebecca.

"Shastekae," said Uncle Rain breathlessly.

Everyone gasped.

"Yeah, he makes swords," said Rebecca.

"And he was attacked by the Vieniem leader," said Aliza.

"AND HE'S THE VIENIEM LEADER'S BROTHER!" exclaimed Daniel.

"NO! IT WASN'T MY SHASTEKAE!" yelled Sweetheart furiously.

"Then where is he?" said Uncle Rain with a frown.

Everyone looked around.

"WHERE IS TANOMI?" thundered Leo.

They all started to panic.

Suddenly, a dark shadow came over them.

They looked up and saw Shastekae is his Lemption form, but this time they saw that he had Vieniem bat wings and an evil grin.

SHASTEKAE

"Looking for me?" called Shastekae.

"Shastekae, Don't Do This? You're Better That Baby!" yelled Sweetheart in tears.

"I'M NOT YOUR BABY WITCH! I'M NOT EVEN YOUR FRIEND! I NEVER LIKED YOU! YOU'RE SUCH AN IDIOT!" yelled Shastekae evilly.

Sweetheart fell to the ground on her knees in tears.

"But This Is Going To Be A Nice Prize!" said Shastekae, as he pulled Taomi's body from behind him; or who she used to be.

She was unconscious.

They could also see Tanomi's hair was no longer brown, but black. Along with her ears that were no longer blue, but were red. She was also wearing a black dress and red fish net stockings, as well as, black high heel shoes with Lemption skull gemmed buckles.

"TAOMI, WAKE UP!" screamed Leo.

"To Late! I've already injected her with Killaim's blood! SHE'LL ALWAYS BE EVIL, SIDE BY SIDE, WITH ME AND MY SISTER," echoed Shastekae.

"Taomi!" screamed Leo even louder.

"She's no longer called Taomi, but 'The Empress of Death,'" said Shastekae with a menacing laugh.

"NOOOOO!" screamed Sweetheart.

"SHUT UP, WITCH! AND YOU'RE NO LONGER MY WIFE! THE EMPRESS OF DEATH IS MY TRUE WIFE! SO BE GONE!" said Shastekae.

"MY SISTER ISN'T YOUR WIFE! NOW EAT BULLETS!" yelled Naomi.

Naomi reached for a gun from a pocket in her belt, and then pointed it up at the evil Shastekae. The guns were given to her ealier by Uncle Rain before their journey.

Then Shastekae put Taomi's body in front of him.

"DON'T SHOOT OR YOU'LL KILL YOUR SISTER TOO!" yelled Shastekae with evil laugh.

"YOU EVIL JERK! LET HER GO! NOW!" screamed Naomi.

"NEVER NAOMI! HA, HA, HA! SHE'LL NEVER REMEMBER YOU FROM NOW ON!" laughed Shastekae evilly, as he flew away from them.

Then everyone ran after him.

Suddenly, he disappeared threw the dark clouds.

Chapter 31

The Scroll and the Yemuel Crystal Holds What Secret

Everyone in the crowd was in panic. They were crying, yelling, and some of them were sobbing on their knees.

"ENOUGH!" echoed Uncle Rain.

He got everyone's attention.

"What are we to do? He has my sister," cried Naomi.

"And he's killed mine," sobbed Tigerisa.

Naomi and Tigerisa embraced each other in sorrow.

Everyone looked hopelessly to each other.

"This isn't fair! Ashley and Leonard could go after him," said Gabriella suddenly.

"We can't," said Leonard.

"Why not?" asked Daniel shocked.

"Well...when lived in the tribe, our tribe was punished for not destroying a group of Lemptions. We...unlike the other Vieniem have adored Lemptions. We thought of them as our kind, as family. BUT WE NEVER TOLD THE REST OF OUR KIND THAT! So our punishment was having all of our wings smashed by stones," explained Ashley sadly.

"But your wings look fine," said Rebecca.

"Our bones healed, but our muscles are permanently torn. So we can't fly," said Leonard.

"Then how come your tribe got destroyed?" asked Gabriella.

"Well later on...some of tribe secretly helped another group of Lemption's get into the tower to get the Reinstone and the Secret Scroll. Some of Killaim's guards came to our tribe to investigate and found that we had smuggled maps of the tower's entry ways and tunnels. Then they found some of us illegally left the camp, so Killiam issued that we all be killed," said Ashley sadly.

"Then how did you get away?" asked Rebecca.

"We were following the group or the last of the group, along with Alexander's step parents. We watched as they were attacked at a cave. There was nothing we could do, or else the Lemption's in the group would know we were helping them. They also would have caught the rest of us. Including, a Lemption girl infant we had found in an empty boat by a river bank, which is the same boat she was sitting in in the picture on the wall in the mansion," said Leonard with a frown.

"But when the Lemption group was attacked at the cave. There was nothing we could do, except watch. There was one Lemption that was bitten and fell off a cliff, and another, who we think was a Lemption, who escaped with the Rhinestone crystal, scroll, and a Lemption infant. Once the evil Vieniems left the sight we went to investigate...And that's when we found Alexander. So we couldn't go back to our tribe because of the slaughter. So since we couldn't go back, we searched for a safe area in the forest of sorrow and built the mansion and toke care of Alexander and his soon to be wife," said Ashley sadly.

"So We Found All Those Maps And Leads From You Vieniems!" said Uncle slowly.

"We tried to not make your finds obvious that we were giving them to you," said Ashley.

"OBSURD!" yelled Uncle Rain.

"Oh really! Then why haven't you've given the Chosen One the secret of the scroll?" asked Leonard.

Suddenly, Uncle Rain went silent.

"What scroll?" asked Aliza curiously.

"Well...remember that scroll I gave you along with those pictures of your Mom and Dad and the Reinstone crystal," said Uncle Rain slowly.

"Yes, what about it? I left it at the cottage," asked Aliza.

"Well... when I grabbed the Rhinestone from the cottage. I also grabbed the scroll," said Uncle Rain.

"What's so important about it?" asked Aliza.

Aliza was a little mad, because her Uncle welcomed himself into her cottage without her permission.

"Since you're the chosen one, your supposed to be the only one who can read the old ancient writing imprinted in this scroll," said Uncle Rain firmly.

He pulled an old rolled up scroll from his back pocket and handed it to Aliza.

When she opened the scroll there was ancient writing quelled on the old paper.

As she starred into the paper her eyes started to glow a bright purple, then red, and then blue.

Suddenly, the crest in her chest shot out a long gold light into the scroll, and the paper scroll began to glow.

Everyone watched in silence and amazement.

Aliza's feet left the ground, as her body showered in gold light.

Aliza's hair waved in the gold light and the glow of her eyes continued changing color.

Then the glowing scroll was absorbed into the crest and Aliza closed her eyes.

Suddenly, Aliza's body had transformed before their eyes.

Aliza's tail, fur, hair, wings emitted gold light and Aliza's body became ten feet tall and her stomach firmed out, while still pregnant. Then her clothes turned into a long gold glowing dress with a slit at the bottom with enough room at the top of the dress to show the Yemuel crystal crest.

ALIZA'S FINAL TRANSFORMATION

Aliza's form was ten feet off the ground in an orb of gold.

Suddenly, she spoke, "Shalah emttew aleheav glavekiaso."

Everyone looked and listened in amazement.

"What did she say?" asked Daniel.

"I don't know. I wonder...if...she's speaking ancient Lemption language that was spoken on Planet Lempton a long time ago, before your planet was destroyed," said Uncle Rain.

Suddenly, her eyes shot gold strings of light.

The strings of light twisted and turned around the group and suddenly shot right into Alexander's eyes. Alexander suddenly floated off the ground into the gold orb Aliza was in with no motion.

Aliza then spoke again, "Sakae rica havite grabae skeetica!"

"What did she say?" said Daniel.

"Do Not Worry Friend's Of The Chosen One, She Will Protect You!" echoed Alexander's voice, still with the string of light still connected from his eyes and Aliza's.

"HOW WILL YOU PROTECT US MISTER ROMANCE WITH THE TOUGH GIRL!? MISTER I'M SO SPECIAL I CAN MAKE A LITTLE SQEEKY TOY BITE YOUR HEAD OFF!" teased Daniel.

Aliza spoke again, "VASLIE MIDISA KILSADIA SOAIDA FIJSA PESEMIA!"

"What Are You Saying? We can't u-n-d-e-r-s-t-a-n-d you!" called Daniel slowly.

WACK!

Rebecca hit Daniel in the head with a nearby medium sized log.

Daniel was now face first in the dirt.

"THE CHOSEN ONE HAS SAID, THE VIENIEMS AND KILLIAM WILL SOON HAVE PEACE WITH US," echoed Alexander.

Daniel got up slowly off of the ground and yelled, "WHAT! HAVE PEACE! YEAH RIGHT! HAVE PIECES OF OUR BODIES AND THE REST OF OUR KIND SITTING ON A PLATTER! STUPID!"

Suddenly, Alexander's body was immersed in gold light and evolved into his true Lemption form. Alexander's body was growing ten feet taller then his actual size, as well as growing gold glowing fur and tail. His face evolved into a cat-like werewolf face, wide jaw, white fangs and claws and slit pupil surround by bright blue iris in the eyes. His shirt and pants became gold and flawless, except for the shoes on his feet where his back claws were so huge to where no shoe would be able to fit.

Kim watched in amazement as her true love became the Chosen One's side kick. She still couldn't believe Alexander was Aliza's brother.

"Seefke lita meekae siftia mikia!" continued Aliza with her wings spread around her.

"There's noting to fear, for the Yemuel Crest and the Rein Stone of Light will protect all who stay within boundaries of this gold orb, which will provide invisibility and a shield up to fifteen feet around the perimeter of it," said Alexander calmly.

"Well, that's a relief," said Ashley with a sigh of relief.

"Why's that?" asked Uncle Rain suspiciously.

"Because with all this light, it will alarm Killaim's Minion's of our presents! We're not that far from the Cliffs and Mountains of Chaos. About ten or fifteen miles I'd say," said Leonard.

"What about Shastekae? He knows where we are!" panicked Daniel loudly.

WACK!

Rebecca slapped Daniel in the back of the head.

"We're Invisible Stupid!" yelled Rebecca angrily.

"SHHHHH...This is protection for invisibility, NOT SOUNDPROOFING!" yelled Uncle Rain quietly.

Suddenly, Aliza and Alexander came out of the gold orb and came to the ground, while the gold light broke between their eyes. The gold orb was still above them. Aliza and Alexander were still glowing gold and in their chosen forms.

Aliza's sword was no longer black, but had a silvery gold blade and the handle was completely made of the Rhinestone's unbreakable crystal.

Aliza and Alexander were at the front of the group.

"Lifae domroe Kotae lierue!" said Aliza, as she spook in the ancient Lemption language.

"We Must Move Quickly! Killaim and her followers are planning their attack as we speak!" said Alexander.

"What About My Wife!?" said Leo furiously.

"And my husband," sniffed Sweetheart, still with tears in her eyes.

"Who cares? He killed my Sister!" exclaimed Tigerisa furiously.

"HE DIDN'T MEAN IT!" cried Sweetheart in tears.

"What! Are you crazy!? He's a complete Vieniem! He even stole Naomi's already married sister as his own wife! Are You stupid! HE DOESN'T CARE ABOUT YOU ANY MORE!" said Gabriella angrily.

"YES, HE DOES CARE ABOUT ME, HE DOES.... THAT'S WHY HE MARRIED ME!" exclaimed Sweetheart, as she bursted into louder tears.

Then Sweetheart pointed to her married earring that Shastekae gave to her at their wedding.

"HE STILL CARES!!!" screamed Sweetheart, still pouring tears.

"Forget it! He only married you because you gave him the puppy eyes! He even said that as you dragged him down the wedding aisle! The love wasn't real!" said Daniel, as he shrugged he shoulders inconsiderately.

Sweetheart's face was buried in her hands crying and fell to her knees.

Suddenly, she brought her face out of her hands and her eyes began to glow a bright reddish pink.

Sweetheart stomped with rage toward Daniel who was staring at the ground not realizing that he was in trouble, as Rebecca happily watched.

WACK! BOOM!

Sweetheart hit Daniel through a trunk of a tree and into the ground.

Daniel had his head sticking out of the ground.

"OUCH! WHAT WAS THAT FOR?" exclaimed Daniel.

"THINK BEFORE YOU SPEAK, DAN!" growled Sweetheart, as she starred him down.

Rebecca walked over with a smile on her face.

"You can plant him in the dirt, but I doubt he'll grow a brain," said Rebecca.

Daniel crawled slowly from in the dirt and got on his feet.

Daniel then spit on to the ground and found on the ground one of his teeth.

"OH MAN!" said Daniel, as he picked up the tooth.

"SKOYO MENTIA SUFAVI!" said Aliza, as she strongly lifted her sword above her head.

Daniel noticed how close he was to Aliza's sword and through himself to the ground.

"SHE'S GOING TO CHOP MY HEAD OFF!" yelled Daniel, as he quickly crawled on the ground and kissed Aliza foot.

She looked down and shook her head.

"SKOYO MENTIA SUFAVI!" said Aliza again strongly and brought her sword down in front of Daniel.

Daniel started to panic.

"PLEASE DON'T KILL ME, I HAVE A WIFE I DEEPLY LOVE AND CHERISH! SHE NEEDS ME!" exclaimed Daniel.

Rebecca shook her head, and said, "YOU'RE PATHETIC!"

"IT'S OKAY, FINISH HIM OFF! I'LL SUVIVE WITH OUT HIM!" called Rebecca with an evil smirk.

"ALIZA SAID, 'THAT'S EHOUGH! WE MOVE ON NOW!'" yelled Alexander firmly.

Then they all headed for the Cliffs and Mountains of Chaos, being led by Aliza and Alexander.

Chapter 32

Feathers Fly

Aliza and the group were walking further and further through thick foliage of gloomy dark creepy plants for about four whole hours.

"Why hasn't the sun come up?" asked Daniel with a yawn.

"SOON KAE MEATIA COMAE!" said Aliza quietly.

"We've come closer to the cliffs and mountains of chaos, it is always dark," said Alexander even quieter.

"How does she know all this?" asked Uncle Rain out loud to himself.

"Because of the scroll it holds an incredible amount of knowledge, but I think she can only tap into only some of the knowledge," whispered Leonard slowly.

"Why only some?" asked Uncle Rain quietly.

"I don't know only some of the older Lemptions know these secrets," whispered Leonard.

THUD!

"OUCH!"

Daniel ran into a tree.

"You idiot. Watch what you're doing," said Rebecca annoyed.

"I would if I could," said Daniel, as he rubbed his head.

"Shhh...you two," said Uncle Rain quietly.

Suddenly, some dark figures flew over them.

It was two Vieniems.

"Oh no, we're in trouble," said Daniel.

"We're invisible, now shut up! They could hear us," said Rebecca quietly.

As they kept walking, they came in between tall rock stone walls.

"SEELOR OMAE TOEL REWEEF!" said Aliza firmly.

"They're Killaim's guards...we're only three miles away. We'll see much more...that means more quiet," said Alexander.

"How are we to fight, we have no weapons. How are to protect ourselves? said Daniel.

"IMORA GALLISANE MIDRIA," said Aliza.

"WHY DON'T YOU SPEAK ENGLISH WOMAN?" said Daniel angrily.

WHAM! THUD!

Daniel was hit in the back of the head by Alexander.

"QUIET! Aliza has a gift for each one of you, but you can only use it once," said Alexander quietly.

Aliza then pulled several golden feathers from the bottom of her wings, and gave one to each person in the group.

"MORYIA SOFEE DOMAE MIA!" said Aliza.

"What did she say?" asked Daniel rubbing his head.

"She said each feather holds the power to grant one wish you happen to make, but it can't bring back the dead," said Alexander.

"Alright!" exclaimed Daniel excitedly.

"Don't waste your gift! You only get one!" said Alexander.

Daniel then looked at his feather with a straight face and then slowly closed his eyes.

Then the feather in his hand dissolved in the air.

"Did you already make your wish?" asked Uncle Rain surprised.

"Yes," said Daniel.

"So what did you wish for? Brains!" teased Rebecca.

"Shut up, you don't need to know what I wished for woman!" said Daniel bothered.

"Fine," said Rebecca.

"So I can't wish for my sister back," asked Tigerisa with her eyes filling with hopeful tears.

Aliza looked at Alexander with a frown. Then Alexander turned to Tigerisa and slowly shook his head.

Tigerisa's eyes then filled with tears, as she looked at the golden feather in her hand.

"Then why didn't you give this to us earlier?" asked Tigerisa angrily.

"She wouldn't be able to be saved. She was crystallized by Shastekae's sword, her death wouldn't of been able to be stopped," said Alexander.

"Why wouldn't she be able to survive?" asked Tigerisa fuming.

"The sword was made out of Lemption crystals, which happen to hold the soul's of previous Lemption's who were killed and their howl's power becomes incased in the Lemption crystal. And when a Lemption crystal is used to cut an object, the object of which it cuts turns into crystal called crystal's death bed in-casing, which can not be reversed," said Alexander.

Tigerisa then buried her face in her hands, fell to her knees, and bursted in to tears.

"What's that sound?" said a hissing voice in the distance.

"Quiet!" said Uncle Rain.

Tigerisa quickly sniffed up her tears, wiped the tears off her face, and stood slowly on her feet.

"Who is it?" whispered Daniel, as he leaned against the cliff side.

Uncle Rain quickly pulled him off the stone wall.

"What was that for?" whispered Daniel.

"Be careful there are several vines that are set by the Vieniems to snag enemies, trespassers, and prey," said Uncle Rain quietly.

After Daniel turned around, he felt something brush against his leg and he looked down and saw a piece of bark sitting on the ground. As he watched it, moved a little; it went one way then the other. He kept watching intently and then reached out his hand and grabbed the bark and nothing was there.

Suddenly, a vine shot from behind him and grabbed his leg.

SLASH!

Uncle Rain cut the vine with a dagger from his left cargo pants pocket.

"Whew!" said Daniel wiping off his forehead.

"Thanks!" whispered Daniel, as he leaned on the stone wall with his arm again.

"I told you before I packed weapons more than I should have food," Said Uncle Rain.

Suddenly, a vine from the top of the stone wall slithered down and quickly wrapped around his wrist and dragged Daniel upward.

"OH NO!" said Daniel.

Uncle Rain jumped to cut Daniel free and Aliza swished her sword, but the vine was too quick.

The vine carried Daniel all the way over the stone wall.

"There he is. He's the trespasser, He's the one makin' all the ruckus," said a hissing voice.

"The guards have him," said Ashley with a shaky voice.

"What's going to happen to the idiot?" asked Rebecca shaking her head.

"He'll probably be taken to the dungeon," said Leonard slowly.

They walked further along quickly and around a corner to find Daniel being tied up by thick black vine.

"I wouldn't struggle stupid Lemption or the vines will burn your skin and drink your blood," said a fat ugly male Vieniem in black ripped pants.

"My name is Daniel. I could bite and kill you right now if I wanted to," said Daniel bravely.

Rebecca was watching around the corner and her mouth dropped at the display of Daniel's bravery.

"Oh really," said the other skinny male Vieniem in a blue shorts.

Then the skinny Vieniem grabbed one of Daniel's ears and twisted it with all his might.

"AHHHHHHHHHHHHHHH! DAAANG! THAT HURTS!" screamed Daniel in pain.

Finally, the skinny Vieniem let go of his ear.

"If you make anymore smart remarks, you'll lose those ears," said the fat ugly Vieniem with an evil smirk.

Daniel became quiet and turned in the way of the group's and Rebecca's way and gave a hopeless look.

He knew never to give away their position.

AHHHH! STOP!" yelled Daniel.

Daniel was then grabbed by the hair and dragged into a dark cave.

When the group came out of the two stone walls to follow and looked up they could see a castle tower that reached passed the dark clouds and brightened only by the moon light. The width of the Vieniem tower's base was that of a small average island.

"SOLO MIA TAGLA!" whispered Aliza.

"BE CAREFUL AND QUIET, WE WILL GO AFTER HIM!" interpreted Alexander quietly.

So they continued to the cave and followed the guards into the dungeon, which seemed to be the only way into the fortress.

Chapter 33

Cavern Crazy

As the group was following the two Vieniems carrying there prisoner, Daniel, the group noticed how dark and gloom the cavern was. The wind made hollows threw the cave and a muttered high pitch voice in the distance.

"Ahhh! Stop, Pulling My Hair!" growled Daniel angrily.

Then both guard's looked at him with a smile.

"You want us to sssstop pulling your hair?" teased the Vieniems.

"Yes! Please anything, but that," sighed Daniel.

"OUCH! NOT THAT EITHIER!" yelled Daniel.

The Vieniem started pulling him by his ears.

"We can't go in there," said Ashley shaking in fear.

"Why not?" asked Tigerisa.

"We can't be tortured again," said Leonard.

Aliza looked to Alexander and nodded.

"It's okay. You can leave, we understand," said Alexander.

"I'm sorry," said Ashley.

"It's okay," said Rebecca.

Then Ashley and Leonard went back the way they came and left.

They finally came to halt because the Vieniem gaurds came to a small cell that smelled like dead fish.

"You're going in here, chump," said the fat Vieniem.

Then they ripped off the vines and threw him in the dark small cell.

Daniel looked behind him there was nothing, but pitch black in the back of the cell.

Then Daniel panicked and grabbed on the bars, as the Vieniems were leaving.

"YOU CAN'T LEAVE ME HERE! I'M AFRAID OF THE DARK!" yelled Daniel.

The Vieniems just laughed in the distance.

"DON'T WORRY YOUR NOT ALONE!" called the fat Vieniem.

"WHAT DO YOU MEAN I'M NOT ALONE?" cried Daniel pitifully.

Suddenly, Daniel heard a rustle in the pitch black of endless darkness in the back of the cell.

Daniel brought out his claws.

"You'd better run! I've got sharp claws and I'm not afraid to use them!" exclaimed Daniel, as his knees were shaking.

Suddenly, he heard something rustle behind him and he turned, but nothing was there.

Daniel was shaking in fear and developed a cold sweat.

Then the rustle was right next to him.

When he turned there was a small dark figure right in front of him with glowing green eye and suddenly disappeared.

Suddenly, arms are wrapped around his body and Daniel noticed it was another Lemption, but younger.

"What The Heck Is Going On? Let go of me!" said Daniel scared half to death.

"I've Been Missing You So Much!" cried the young Lemption.

"WHAT AM I? YOUR MOTHER!" yelled Daniel.

"I Know You'd Come Back For Me Mommy," said the young Lemption in joy.

"Get away from me you idiot," said Daniel, as he squeezed from the young Lemption's grip.

Suddenly, Rebecca came into view.

"Get back into the protection!" said Daniel.

"Aliza, said it was safe," said Rebecca.

"Is she finally speaking English?" asked Daniel.

"Yes, she found it would be easier for us to communicate. She also allowed herself to become our size still in her gold chosen form…and Alexander is back to his normal self," explained Rebecca.

"Thank goodness you're here. Get me away from this idiot," said Daniel desperately

Rebecca turned to see the other younger Lemption sitting on the ground behind Daniel, who was picking his nose, and flicked a bugger on the wall of the cell.

"Wow, he's got a better I.Q. then you," said Rebecca with a smile.

"SHUT UP WOMAN!" said Daniel.

"Okay then, will have a contest to see who's smarter? What's two plus two?" said Rebecca.

"FOUR!" exclaimed the young Lemption in the cell.

"NO WAY! IT'S TWO!" yelled Daniel.

Rebecca turned away and shook her head.

"You're the idiot," said Rebecca.

The young Lemption in the cell sniffed the air.

"I smell my mommy!" said the young Lemption.

"I'm not your stupid mother, idiot," exclaimed Daniel.

"Then why do I smell her?" asked the young Lemption with watery puppy eyes.

"Then what's her name?" asked Rebecca.

"NAMOMMY!" said the young Lemption.

Naomi realized the voice and the close mention of her name from outside the shield and turned from behind the group to get a better look at who spoke. She noticed his black ears (of which one was half gone), light purple hair, and green eyes.

Naomi stepped out of the protective shield slowly and walked over to the younger Lemption, who was further back in the cave.

"Jonathan...is that you?" asked Naomi slowly.

"Mommy," said the Lemption, as he turned around with hopeful eyes.

The young Lemption ran over to Naomi and started to cry. They embraced each other between the bars.

"Mommy, I knew you'd find Me," cried Jonathan.

"My Jonathan," cried Naomi.

"He's your son?" said Daniel in awe.

"Yes, he's my baby!" exclaimed Naomi, still hugging Jonathan.

She stroked his hair very gently and rocked him back and forth in her arms just barely because the bars were in the way.

"What!? He's so stupid! He's an idiot! He thought I was his mother! Naomi's to hot to be his mother!" said Daniel.

"He's just five years old," said Naomi, as she turned to Daniel with an unexplainable expression of anger.

Naomi stomped over to Daniel towering over him beyond the bars.

"No, no...It's just! I'm sorry...he's Handsome, just like you. I...I mean...uh...uh pretty. You're nice...both...both of you," trembled Daniel, as he backed away from the front of the cell's gate.

WHAM! THUD!

Naomi broke open the gate and reached for Daniel by the collar of his shirt.

"Don't ever talk about my baby like that again," said Naomi, as she pulled him off the ground.

SLAM!

Naomi shoved Daniel's face and body three feet into the ground.

Jonathan giggled.

"The mean boy got beat up by my mommy!" sung Jonathan in a silly tune.

"Exactly my thought," said Rebecca with a smile.

Suddenly, there was light emitting in the dark dungeon through a small opening in the door down where the two Vieniems had previously exited through.

"WHAT'S THAT NOISSSSSE?" exclaimed one of the Vieniem's deep hissing voice.

"HE'SSSS GETTING AWAY!" exclaimed one of the Vieniems, who happened to be looking out of the opening of the door at the end of the row of cells.

Naomi, who was dragging Daniel, also walking with her was Rebecca and Jonathan, as they made their way quickly into Aliza's invisible barrier.

"Hush!" said Naomi, as she held Jonathan close to her.

Suddenly, the two Vieniems dashed out of the door.

"Where did they go?" exclaimed the fat ugly Vieniem.

"Not far, I can sssssmell them," hissed the other Vieniem.

"Check the cell!" said the skinny Vieniem.

The fat ugly Vieniem went inside the cell.

"I don't sssssee anything," said the ugly Vieniem.

Naomi was watching the two evil Vieniems with a furious look fuming in anger because they kept her child locked up for two years.

Suddenly, Naomi shot out of the invisible protection and knocked out both Vieniems.

SLAM!

Naomi through the two Vieniems into a nearby cell and jammed shut the doors of the cell with full force.

Johnathan was amazed at his Mom's strength after not seeing her for two years relentlessly being mistreated by the Vieniem gaurds.

Then the group walked through the open door at the end of the dungeon and found several large stone brick tunnels leading in different directions.

"I'll howl and search each hall way," said Kim quietly.

As she was about to howl, Naomi covered her hand over Kim's mouth.

"Don't howl or you'll give away our position," said Naomi quietly.

"It's too late for that," said a familier voice behind them.

They turned to find Shastekae in his evil form, with Taomi, the dark empress, behind him.

Shastekae's eyes were glowing a green with an evil grin on his face carrying a large sword.

"How can he see us?" whimpered Daniel trembling.

"He's using the power of a crystal," said Aliza firmly.

Aliza stomped one foot on the ground and brought down the protective shield.

"You will not stop us from pursuing our mission," said Aliza.

Everyone hid behind Aliza.

"We'll see about that," said Shastekae.

Shastekae charged with full force with his sword in his hands.

"BACK AWAY!" shouted Aliza.

She raised her hand and then the Yemuel crystal on her chest began to glow a deep blue. Suddenly, a blast of blue light shot from her hand and blasted the sword out of Shastekae's hand.

"How could she do that?" thought Shastekae.

"Wow! You look different. Did you do something to your hair?" said Shastekae with an evil smirk.

Taomi walked next to him.

"Do you love my new look?" said Taomi with a menacing smile.

Taomi had blood red eyes and jet black hair. She had black fangs and silver lips and her hands had black nails. She was wearing a tight black dress that end ended at the very top of her thighs and had red fish net stockings that started right after the end of the bottom of her dress.

"T...Taomi, Is that you?" said Leo walking up to her.

"My name is now Talarka. NOW GET AWAY FROM ME, LOSER!" yelled Talarka, who used to be Tanomi.

She brought out her claws and slashed the side of his face.

Leo backed away pressing his hands against the left side of his face.

Suddenly, blood began to dribble between his paws.

"TAOMI! LISTEN TO ME! I KNOW YOU'RE IN THERE!" yelled Leo, as he reached out for her.

"If you won't get away, fine. Have it your way!" exclaimed Talarka.

Suddenly, Talarka let out a blood curdling howl.

"Let's see you get out of this one fur ball!" said Talarka with an evil smirk.

Suddenly, behind her there were many glowing red eyes with loud growls. When the eyes got closer Leo found that they were huge panthers with drooling jaws of large black teeth.

ONE OF TALARKA'S PANTHERS

"That's new," said Daniel.

One panther jumped at Leo and tried to bite his neck, as the others surrounded him.

Leo tried to hold down the one panther, but he was using all his strength.

"Have Fun Kids!" chuckled Talarka.

Leo jumped as high as he could over the panther to try to stay out of their reach.

Suddenly, two panthers got both of his back feet in each of their mouths.

"Bring him to me!" commanded Talarka.

The two panthers dragged Leo by his bloody feet to her.

"Now you'll find out what it means to feel pain," said Talarka evilly.

"Taomi...please. I...I know you s...still love me," said Leo, as he gritted his teeth in pain.

"Oh really. You still think I'd love a loser like you. You must really be STUPID!" exclaimed Talarka.

"Taomi...please," said Leo quietly.

"Kids," said Talarka, as she looked to the panthers with Leo's feet in their mouths.

CRUNCH!

The panthers bit down hard on Leo's feet.

"AHHHHHHHHHHHH!" screamed Leo.

Blood began to pour out of the two panther's jaws.

Leo fainted.

"Bring him with me!" commanded Talarka.

The two panthers dragged the unconscious Leo down the one tunnel to the left, with Talarka, and the other panthers that followed behind and disappeared in the darkness.

"Isn't she wonderful?" said Shastekae with an evil loving smile.

Everyone had a mortified expression.

"Shastekae! Why would you allow such a thing! I know you're better then this! I know you still have a caring heart within you!" exclaimed Aliza.

She stood in front the whole group with an ashamed expression.

"NO, I DON'T! I ONLY CARE ABOUT KILLAIM AND TALARKA!" yelled Shastekae.

"You still care about us don't you? I can see it in your heart." said Aliza looking deeply in his eyes.

Shastekae's evil eyes widened and then he shook his head, as if he was affected by something..

"NO I DON'T! And if you don't like it...I...I'll kill you myself." stuttered Shastekae.

Chapter 34

Why? Why? Why?

Aliza stood outside surrounded by dead trees with Shastekae across from her.

The group was a distance behind Aliza.

As she stood, the ground below her glowed gold.

"I'll kill you slowly and make you suffer. You'll regret ever saying that I'll ever love any of you," growled Shastekae.

"Shastekae...I know that you still care about us. Especially your wife!" said Aliza calmly.

"HOW DARE YOU!!!" yelled Shastekae.

He leaped in the air and brought his sword down to stab her.

She brought her hand above her quickly and her hand glowed a deep blue as the crest in her chest illuminated a deep blue.

CRASH!!!

Her hand let out blue lighting and hit Shastekae.

Shastekae hit the ground hard.

"Why are you so angry? Sweetheart loves you with all her heart...isn't that enough for you?" said Aliza, as she tilted her head slightly with a frown.

"NO! I HATE HER! SHE'S NOT FOR ME! TALARKA IS! I CARE ABOUT HER!" shouted Shastekae angrily.

Sweetheart was crying immensely and on her knees with her hands covering her eyes.

Naomi came next to her and held close.

"It's okay, nice lady...Don't cry," said Jonhnathan.

He took Sweetheart's hand and started to stroke it.

Sweetheart gave a weak smile and then began to cry again.

Shastekae looked at Sweetheart and then shook his head.

Then he looked at Aliza with an evil grin.

"Let me prove that I hate her!" exclaimed Shastekae.

Shastekae darted for Sweetheart and grabbed her by the neck with one hand and lifted her off the ground.

"I KILL HER INSTEAD!!!" yelled Shastekae angrily.

Sweetheart tried to pull his hand off her neck.

"Shastekae don't. You know you don't have the heart to end her life," said Aliza shaking her head slowly.

Shastekae gave an angry look to Aliza and tightened his grip on Sweetheart's neck.

Sweetheart gagged and had tears roll down cheeks over Shastekae's hand.

Shastekae felt the tears on his hand and looked at Sweetheart.

Suddenly, Shastekae felt his heart strike him weak and dropped Sweetheart to the ground.

Sweetheart breathed heavily with tears falling from her eyes, as she layed on the ground.

"I knew you couldn't kill her. Deep in your heart still holds love for your true mate," said Aliza with a smile.

"DON'T TELL ME WHAT I CAN AND CAN'T DO!" shouted Shastekae.

Shastekae swished his blade in front of him and a large blast of light shot out at Aliza.

The light hit Aliza with huge force.

Sweetheart began to slowly push herself off the ground and looked at where the light was surrounding Aliza's body.

"Aliza...I'm sorry," said Sweetheart quietly with tears falling down her face

Sweetheart thought it was all over for Aliza.

Suddenly, the light surrounding Aliza began to fade away.

Aliza had disappeared.

"WHERE ARE YOU WITCH?!" shouted Shastekae.

"Up here," said Aliza's voice.

Shastekae looked up in the night sky and found Aliza with her wings spread out and flying in the sky.

"Don't seem so surprised," said Aliza calmly, as she slowly flapped her wings.

"How...how did you avoid my light slash!" said Shastekae in a shaky voice.

"I didn't...you missed," said Aliza slowly.

"Fine. BUT I WON'T MISS THIS TIME!!!" yelled Shastekae.

He spread his bat-like wings and shot in the sky toward Aliza's body.

Then he tried to slice her body.

She lowered her body below him.

"You missed...try to aim this time," said Aliza with a weak smile.

"FINE! I'LL SPEAR YOU YOUR BODY!" shouted Shastekae angrily.

He took his sword and through it at Aliza.

"You missed again," said Aliza quickly.

"AHHHHHHHHHHHH!"

Sweetheart had screamed.

Aliza and Shastekae turned quickly in her direction.

"Oh no," said Aliza quietly.

Sweetheart had been hit by the sword.

Aliza had stepped to the ground and began to walk toward Sweetheart's body.

SWISH!

Shastekae had darted passed Aliza and landed next to Sweetheart's body.

Shastekae felt his heart begin to throb and his body began to change into his normal Lemption form.

He had detransformed back into the Lemption form and was no longer The Terror of Death.

"Did he turn back into the good guy?" asked Daniel.

He had hidden behind Uncle Rain the whole time.

The golden feather in Sweetheart blood covered hand had slowly begun to disappear.

"She used her feather from Aliza's wing...to t...turn him n...normal," stuttered Uncle Rain.

"He's a good guy now?" asked Daniel.

"I guess so," whispered Uncle Rain.

Shastekae fell to his knees beside Sweetheart's body.

"no," whispered Shastekae.

Shastekae began to cry.

Sweetheart's body had been pierced by Shastekae's sword in her side.

Shastekae took Sweetheart's blood covered hand in his.

"I...I...I'm so s...sorry," cried Shastekae quietly.

Then he removed the sword and held Sweetheart in his arms.

Everyone around him began to have tears fall down their faces.

Sweetheart's eyes slightly opened and slowly turned her head toward Shastekae.

Shastekae's eyes met hers.

"I'll always...love you," whispered Sweetheart.

"I'll always l...love you too," cried Shastekae quietly.

He kissed her.

"I know you do," said Sweetheart.

Sweetheart's head fell to her side and breathed her last breath.

Sweetheart died.

"Why...WHY? NOOOOOOOOO!" howled Shastekae.

The ground shook violently

Shastekae put Sweetheart to the ground.

Suddenly, her body faded into the ground and flowers immediately grew where she had died.

Shastekae stood up and clenched his fist.

Shastekae's arms and hands were drenched in Sweetheart's blood.

Daniel walked up to him and patted him on the back.

"It's okay," said Daniel.

"No...no it's not," said Shastekae.

"Yep...and it's all your fault," said Daniel.

"I KNOW THAT!!!" screamed Shastekae loudly.

Shastekae punched Daniel in the stomach and he flew sixty yards and then in the side of the castle.

Daniel flopped to the ground unconscious.

Rebecca pulled her hand to her head.

"Idiot," said Rebecca, as she shook her head.

"Shastekae...What do we do now?" asked Tigerisa sadly.

Tigerisa finally realized what Shastekae had done to her sister was nothing but some sort of setup and a major mistake.

"I'll Tell You What We're Going To Do! We're GOING AFTER KILLAIM!" exclaimed Shastekae angrily.

Everyone nodded their heads.

"Let's Go," said Aliza, as she folded her wings.

Chapter 35

To Little, To Late

Aliza was still cloaking the group with the invisibility shield.

Aliza and the group had walked to the end of the tunnel meeting three tunnels going in three different directions. The three tunnels were pitch black inside.

They remembered Talarka, The Empress of Death, having her leopards drag Leo through the tunnel to the left.

"I think I can help," said Gabriella.

"Wow! She spoke!" said Daniel.

"What he means to say is why have you been so quiet?" asked Rebecca.

"I only speak when I am needed," said Gabriella.

She was still holding a glass orb with light emitting from it.

She walked up to the tunnel on the left, which was the same path Talarka had gone through.

Then Gabriella howled, but no one could hear it.

Suddenly, the glass orb in her hands bursted a binding light and the tunnel before her filled with light.

"Wow! How Did She Do That?" exclaimed Daniel.

"I didn't hear her howl," said Rebecca.

"My howl is silent, but inside glass it builds a small sun-like ball inside and it lights up a whole pathway over twenty feet before me," said Gabriella quietly.

"Neat!" said Uncle Rain.

"Very impressive, Gabriella," said Aliza with a smile.

They all started to walk through the left tunnel.

Alexander looked at Kim and found that tears were running down her cheeks and that she was crying silently.

Alexander noticed that she was holding her locket tightly in her hand.

"Kim?" asked Alexander kindly.

"Yes," said Kim turning her head slightly toward him.

"What's in the locket?" asked Alexander slowly.

She opened the locket and showed Alexander what was in it.

Alexander saw a picture of a baby girl Lemption wrapped in a pink blanket and holding a rattle.

The baby girl had brown ears, black hair, and pink eyes, just like Kim.

"Who is she?" asked Alexander slowly.

"She's gone," said Kim sadly.

"How is she gone? What happened to her?" asked Alexander feeling deeply sorry for Kim.

Kim looked at him with watery eyes and looked to the ground as she continued walking.

"Me and my family lived in a small village and my little sister had just been born. We all loved each other very much and lived in a place surrounded by friends. The place we lived in was beautiful and in the distance of the village there was a river that was pure and crystal clear," explained Kim, as she smiled slightly.

"Then what happened?" asked Alexander.

Kim frowned with tears still running down her cheeks.

"I'm sorry. It must be too painful to talk about. Forgive me. Don't worry, I'll be quiet. I won't ask any more questions," said Alexander quickly.

He covered his mouth with his hand.

Kim gave a silent giggle.

"It's okay," said Kim with a small smile.

She continued.

"One day my parents told me to fetch some water from the river and so I took a large jug and went to the river. Then when I was filling the jug I suddenly heard screams from the village and when I turned I saw smoke rising from it. So I immediately ran to the village, but by the time I got there...it was too late. The whole village was burned down and everyone was slaughtered...including my parents...but my sister was gone... and when I found her she was killed," said Kim sadly.

Kim broke down crying in Alexander's arms.

"Did Vieniems kill them?" asked Alexander, as he stroked her hair.

"I d...don't kn...kn...know," choked Kim bursting in tears.

Rebecca over heard the whole conversation and put her hand on Kim's back and hugged her.

Tigerisa walked next to them.

"It's okay, Kim. We all have our sad stories," said Tigerisa, as she patted Kim on the back.

"What happened to all of you before you became the Secret Scouts Six?" asked Rebecca.

"Well...we all came from the same village and we found each other after the disaster...well...except for Gabriella. She was in the forest since she was a baby...abandoned," explained Tigerisa sadly.

They all looked at Gabriella, who was leading them down the tunnel.

"She's the strongest of all of us. We all cry about our past from time to time, but Gabriella never does. She never lets it bother her," said Naomi.

"Mommy, what happened to you?" asked Jonathan holding Naomi's hand.

"I lived in the same village to...but like me and so called Taomi...we were sisters...and...and we were orphans," said Naomi with a sad look.

"Where's your Mommy and Daddy?" asked Jonathan tugging on Naomi's arm.

"We don't know...we never knew," said Naomi, while she shook her head looking blankly in the distance.

Daniel suddenly put his hand on Kim's shoulder.

"It's okay, Kim. I know how you feel," said Daniel with a sad look.

"How do you know how she feels! You Idiot!" said Rebecca, as she raised her hand to strike Daniel's face.

"Because my parents had been killed to. And you've never asked," said Daniel, as he looked straight into Rebecca's eyes.

Rebecca's face went blank and brought her hand down slowly.

"What happened?" asked Rebecca calmly.

" Me and my parents lived in a house in an open field surrounded by a huge forest. I was playing with a toy car and age five at the time and my parents went out to look for food. Before I knew it the house had caught on fire, so I tried to get out of house. Then I found out all the doors and windows had been blocked off. So I went to my room and I saw it was blocked off, but there was a small opening and I looked through it. I saw my parents laying on the ground bleeding to death, and I tried to call out their names to get me out of the house. They tried to crawl to the window where I was at. Then suddenly a stranger blocked part of the window and I only saw my parents. The stranger shot my parents with a gun and killed them. I...I c...couldn't do an... anything," said Daniel, as his eyes filled with tears.

Rebecca was shocked and then hugged Daniel.

Daniel cried silently in her arms, as tears fell down his face.

Daniel let go of his sadness and stepped away from Rebecca.

"You can hit me now, if you want," said Daniel looking at Rebecca.

Rebecca giggled and hugged him again.

"So how did you survive?" asked Naomi curiously.

"I killed all the strangers and destroyed the burning house I was trapped in," said Daniel looking away from them.

Everyone laughed, except for Daniel.

"How?" asked Kim.

"I'd...rather not talk about it," said Daniel looking at the ground.

"Yeah Right! He just got out of the house and ran off!" laughed Tigerisa.

"Yeah, he just escaped without being seen!" exclaimed Kim.

Naomi and Rebecca just stared at Daniel's frown, as he looked at the ground walking.

They knew Daniel was hiding something.

"AHHHHHHHHHHH!!!"

Suddenly, they all were startled.

They heard the familiar loud scream in the distance at the end of the tunnel.

"Turn off the light, Gabriella," said Aliza suddenly, as she walked in front of her.

Gabriella made a silent howl again and the light diminished.

They walked to the end of the tunnel and peaked around the edge.

They saw Leo covered in blood being held down to the ground by Talarka's panthers.

Talarka was standing in a huge stone room. The room was over twenty yards wide and fifty feet tall and the doom like ceiling was stain glass in the colors of purple, blue, and red circles. It was lit by large red pillar candles, flicking light on the walls of the room. The floor of the stone room was made of wide black square tiles and in a glassy shine slightly covered by dust.

Talarka was pacing in front of Leo.

"Now again...where did they go and where is my husband...he disappeared along with those good for nothings. I can no longer smell his decent Vieniem contaminated blood," said Talarka, as she stopped pacing and stood towering in over Leo's body.

"I...I...I don't kn...know," said Leo gritting his teeth.

Shastekae had uncomfortable chills go up his spine at what he heard come out of Talarka's mouth.

Leo was in immense pain and trying to pull away from the panthers.

Talarka snapped her fingers.

"AHHHHHHHHH!
AHHHHHHHHHHHHHHHHHHHHHHHH!"

The panthers crushed the bones in Leo's arms with they're jaws.

"Again...Where Are They?!" shouted Talarka angrily.

"I DON'T KNOW!" screamed Leo crying in pain.

Talarka snapped her fingers again.

"AHHHHHHHHHHHHH!"
"AHHHHHHHHHHHHHHHHHHHHHHHHHH!"

The panthers crushed Leo's legs in they're jaws. Leo was now in a puddle of blood and suffering from blood loss.

"AGAIN, WHERE ARE THEY?!" yelled Talarka furiously.

"I told you...I don't know," panted Leo.

"THAT'S IT! DESTROY HIM!" shouted Talarka, as she walked out of the large room.

"AHHHHHHHHH! AHHHHHHHHHHHHH! STOP! NOOOOOOOOOOOOOO! AHHHHHHHHHHHHHH!"

The panther were tearing apart Leo's limbs and scratching in him deeply in the face and back.

Aliza and the group darted for Leo and Aliza brought down the shield.

As soon as the panthers saw them, they left Leo and ran towards them ready to tear them apart.

Aliza brought out her hand before her and whispered an unfamiliar word in the ancient Lemption language.

"MEAKIA!"

Suddenly, the crest in her chest glowed and deep blue lighting shot out of her hand and spread about her.

As the light swirled around her each panther was hit and thrown into the air.

When the panthers were in the air Aliza whispered another ancient word.

"STARIA!"

Then the crest glowed gold and blinding gold wind began to swirl above her, blowing through her hair.

Then Aliza raised her hand from where she had it and whispered another ancient word.

"SEFOE!"

Then the wind hit the panthers.

Suddenly, the wind threw them to the ground and pushed them into the ground beneath them and suffocated them.

Suddenly, the tiles cracked along the floor.

The panthers were pushed by the wind almost three feet into the stone tile floor and stopped struggling.

Aliza threw her hand to her side and the gold wind disappeared.

Then she walked to where the panthers were laying and found them dead.

Aliza nodded her head and walked toward the group.

"Amazing...I never knew such power," whispered Uncle Rain to himself.

The groups stood stunned at what Aliza had done and were speechless.

Aliza then walked toward Leo's mauled body.

"Help...help her...help Taomi...from the evil that possesses her...help her," said Leo weakly.

Aliza kneeled beside him and placed her hand gently on a spot of his head that had not been injured.

"You can. Use the feather I gave you and use the power to release her from the grasp of Killaim's poisoned blood," said Aliza kindly.

Leo suddenly choked deathly and rested his head on the ground and the feather that he still had hidden in his grip faded away.

Suddenly, Leo stopped breathing and died.

Everyone began to cry at the loss of another one of their comrades.

Aliza stood on her feet and looked to where Talarka had left.

"Come. We must move on and stop this calamity before anymore lives are lost," said Aliza, as she walked following Talarka's path.

Everyone nodded to each other and began to follow Aliza.

Chapter 36

The Changes

Aliza and the group were now making their way up a swirling stone stair case that began at the end of the tunnel. The stairs went up fifty feet along a stone wall and the stair case only had a small flimsy wire rail.

"Don't look down," said Alexander with a shaky voice.

Daniel looked down and his heart stopped. They were over thirty feet above a hard stone floor.

"That's a terrifying drop!" exclaimed Daniel, who was scared and shaking.

Each stair was just a brick that extended out of the wall.

The stairs shook every time one of them took a step.

Aliza was in the front and next was Gabriella, then Uncle Rain, then Jonathan, then Naomi, then Tigerisa, then Shastekae, then Rebecca, then Alexander, then Kim, and then Daniel.

"AND WHY AM I IN THE END OF THE GROUP!" exclaimed Daniel with a shaky voice.

"Because if a Vieniem comes up behind us we want you to be the first to go!" yelled Rebecca angrily.

"Ah, how settle," said Shastekae to himself.

"Shut up!" yelled Rebecca, even more angrily.

Kim giggled.

E. A. Andersen

"And what are you laughing about! That's not funny! Move! I'm getting in front of you!" yelled Daniel, as he tried to push Kim to the side.

Suddenly, the weight under both Kim and Daniel pressed heavily on the stone step beneath them.

"AHHHHHHH!"

"AHHHHHH!"

The step broke and Daniel and Kim began to fall.

Aliza spread her wings and dived down to catch Kim and Daniel, but she couldn't because they were falling so fast.

They were about to hit the stone floor.

"They're not going to survive if they hit the floor!!!" screamed Alexander.

Suddenly, Rebecca howled.

The gravity disappeared and everyone began to float in mid air.

Kim and Daniel never hit the ground and were floating above the stone floor.

"WHY DIDN'T YOU USE THIS WHEN WE FIRST FELL!? YOU IDIOT!" screamed Daniel to Rebecca.

Rebecca suddenly jumped off the wall with full strength and shot down toward Daniel.

Rebecca was hurling toward him at full speed with her fist ready to strike.

"Uh oh," whispered Daniel to himself.

BOOM!

Rebecca punched Daniel in the head and he slammed hard on stone floor.

"Ouch!" said Uncle Rain.

Daniel was still conscious, but had a large lump on his head.

Kim used her legs and leaped up to the steps to Alexander.

"Oh, thank goodness you're okay. I was so worried." said Alexander, as he embraced her in his arms.

Kim then peaked a kiss on Alexander's cheek.

"I didn't mean to worry you," giggled Kim.

Alexander blushed.

Everyone laughed.

"Enough, let's continue!" exclaimed Aliza kindly.

"Use your feet to reach the top!" called Rebecca.

Everyone leaped off the walls to the top and landed on the ground in the next stone tunnel.

Rebecca howled again and the gravity came back.

Everyone touched to the ground with their feet.

THUD!

Daniel landed face first in the ground.

Everyone laughed.

"I sense danger," said Aliza looking around her.

"Ha! So we meet again!" called a familiar voice in the distance of the pitch black tunnel.

The stranger came out of the shadows before them.

It was Killaim.

Chapter 37

Going down with the Wind

The group was standing in the stone tunnel where Killaim was smirking evilly at them.

"So...I didn't expect you were coming. I thought you'd be a cowardly rat crawling back your hole with your tail between your legs," chucked Killaim, as she drew a large sword from a black leather pack on her back.

The sword had a sharp silver Lemption crystal blade with a gold handle.

"Who made that sword?" asked Naomi, as she walked past Aliza.

"Oh...this. Well, thanks to The Terror of Death who you now seem to call Shastekae. He gladly made this weapon for me. Thanks Shastekae!" said Killaim with another evil smile.

Shastekae buried his face in his hands.

"That's not fair! You made him that monster!" yelled Rebecca angrily.

"I did didn't I. Well...he's my insolent brother...what did you expect." said Killaim.

"You're not evil...you only choose to be. I can see right through you...Killaim." said Aliza frowning at her.

"Well, your sadly mistaken." yelled Killaim angrily.

Killaim spread her wings angrily and as she spread them they began to pulse a deep red. Then she charged at Aliza at full speed holding her sword above head ready to strike Aliza.

Aliza threw her hand before her.

"MEKI!"

Aliza had again spoken an ancient word from the Lemption language.

Killaim froze in her position.

Killaim tried to move, but her body wouldn't listen.

"GILA!"

Aliza shouted another unfamiliar ancient Lemption word.

Killaim's body flew back over ten meters and knocked the wind out of her.

"In all the foes I've faced! I never..," shouted Killaim angrily.

"Surprised! You'll never beat Aliza! She's to strong! You're such a weakling, you stupid bat!" teased Daniel.

"Hush, Daniel!" said Aliza, as she turned to look at him.

"Sorry." said Daniel ashamed.

WACK!

"Ouch!" yelled Daniel.

Rebecca hit him hard on the head.

SLAM!

Killaim hit Aliza hard with her body.

Aliza was thrown into the wall of the stone tunnel.

"DON'T IGNORE ME! YOU FEATHERED FLAKE!" yelled Killaim angrily.

Aliza stood up strongly, as if nothing happened.

"Your so angry...you need to find peace in your heart," said Aliza calmly as she turned back to Killaim.

"Rrrrrrr...You need to shut up!" screamed Killaim, as she charged at Aliza again with her sword.

Aliza threw her hand up again.

"GILA!"

Aliza spoke the ancient word again.

Suddenly, Killaim used her wings and flew over where Aliza's hand was pointed.

Killaim wasn't thrown back.

Aliza was surprised at Killaim's ability to avoid her attack.

Killaim flapped her red pulsing wings hard and shot at Aliza to slice her body with the sword.

"MEKI!"

Aliza shouted another ancient word with her hand aimed at Killaim again.

Killaim froze in mid air.

"Stop fighting your feelings, Killaim!" said Aliza slowly.

Killaim fell from her frozen position and hit the ground hard.

Killaim looked up at Aliza with disgust.

Suddenly, Naomi stepped in front of Aliza with the two guns she had and pointed them at Killaim.

"Don't worry! I'll take care of her!" exclaimed Naomi.

Killaim hissed loudly at them.

Suddenly, Killaim dashed into the darkness before Naomi could take a shot.

Naomi, Aliza, and the rest of the group ran after her.

They came up right near Killaim who was standing and smirking at them.

"PREPARE TO DIE, KILLAIM!" shouted Naomi, as she aimed her guns at Killaim's body.

Suddenly, the whole group saw that Killaim was holding Talarka's body in front of her in the way of Naomi's aim.

Talarka had transformed back into Taomi. She had blue ears and a blue tail again with her normal brown hair.

Taomi was unconscious.

"You care to explain this...Aliza. How have you been reversing my blood's effect?" said Killaim.

"Your poison isn't really evil...your poison is just filled with your anger and hate. My power of the Yemuel crystal was bonded to the secret scroll which came from our planet. The Chosen Lemption that is born after so many generations has a Yemuel crystal born in her body, but the power can only be released if the scroll of the Vieniems and the Yemuel crystal of the Lemptions are combined. I reversed your poison with these combined powers to pure our rivalry between our species. Your heart isn't really evil... it is just confused because of what happened to your parents and because of our generation's history. Your mother really wanted to make these changes and that is how she was able to fall in love with a Lemption. She wanted you to love Lemptions too and make peace between our races also. But things changed that...I am sure that your father didn't really kill your mother. We need to help each of our species and stop this slaughter...and end this need to kill....Killaim." explained Aliza firmly.

Killaim threw Taomi in front of her.

"You need to shut up." said Killaim starring at the ground.

They all saw tears starting to roll down her cheeks.

"DON'T EVER SPEAK OF MY MOTHER AGIAN! YOU BEAST!" screamed Killaim furiously.

Killaim spread her wings violently and shot into in air.

"STAY AWAY FROM ME!!!" screamed Killaim as she flew as fast as she could down the tunnel away from them.

Naomi ran to Taomi's body.

"SISTER! SISTER! WAKE UP! WAKE UP, TAOMI!" shouted Naomi with tears falling from her eyes.

Suddenly, Taomi's eyes opened a little.

"Sister...Naomi...is that you?" asked Taomi quietly.

"You're okay!" said Naomi, as she hugged Taomi.

"Where's Leo, Naomi?" asked Taomi quietly.

"He's...h...he's d...dead, sister." choked Naomi sadly.

Taomi stood up quickly.

"D...de...dead h...how?" asked Taomi stuttering with tears starting to river down her face.

"Hi Taomi. Welcome back. You killed Leo with your panthers remember!" said Daniel.

Taomi put her hands on Naomi's shoulders and looked into Naomi's sad eyes.

"Please...please...p...please tell m...me that n...not true." cried Taomi quietly.

Naomi looked into Taomi's tear filled eyes and nodded.

"NOOOOOOOO!" screamed Taomi.

Taomi fell to her knees with her face buried in her hands and bursted into tears.

"Ooops." said Daniel.

"YOUR SUCH A MORON!" yelled Rebecca.

WHAM! CRASH!

Rebecca slammed Daniel into the wall and punched him in the back.

"YOU NEVER CONSIDER OTHER PEOPLE'S FEELINGS! IDIOT!" yelled Rebecca.

WHAM! WHAM! CRASH!

Rebecca threw Daniel into the wall twice and kicked him in the butt.

"WHY DON'T YOU THINK BEFORE YOU SPEAK? STUPID!" yelled Rebecca.

WHAM! WHAM! WHAM! WHAM! WHAM! CRASH!

Rebecca hit Daniel's head into the stone wall five times and then punched in the face.

"Rebecca, give the guy a break." said Tigerisa with a chuckle.

"Y...yeah...please give me a break, Rebecca." coughed Daniel.

"Oh okay...okay fine. I'll give you a break." said Rebecca.

CRUNCH!

"AHHHHHHHHHHHHHHHHHHHH!" screamed Daniel.

Rebecca used her knee on Daniel's elbow and pulled his arm backwards, breaking his arm.

"Humph." huffed Rebecca, as she turned and walked away from Daniel's helpless body on the ground.

Rebbeca finally had it with Daniel's incompetent, ignornant, and disrespectful comments.

"Ouch." said Uncle Rain.

"Rebecca...that's not what I meant when I said give him a break." said Tigerisa with a frown.

"He was asking for it." said Rebecca.

Everyone shook their heads.

Uncle Rain took a white towel out of his pack and splinted Daniel's arm.

Daniel let out a weak sad sigh and got to his feet.

"Okay, then...we must continue." said Aliza, as she walked in the direction that Killaim flew away.

Everyone nodded their heads and followed Aliza.

Chapter 38

Gone Missing?

Aliza and the group had reached the final end of the stone tunnels and met a huge room. The room had gray marble-like ceramic floors with cracks in them and stone walls and huge pillars. The room was dark and was only lit in certain areas by little fire candles. The pillars were so tall that even the ceiling was unable to see.

"It's to dark in there let's go back," said Daniel, who was chilled by the empty darkness.

The room went on through the darkness, so they couldn't see where it ended.

"There's no where else to continue from, we have to go through this room. So let's stick together closely," said Aliza.

"Wait! Gabriella, can't you use your glowing orb?" asked Tigerisa.

"I can't," said Gabriella.

"Why not?" asked Rebecca.

"Because of the fire lit candles. My orb of light can cause them to ignite in huge flames and possibly set this room and us on fire," said Gabriella firmly.

"I see," said Naomi.

"And How Is That!?" exclaimed Daniel.

"None of your business," said Rebecca, as she raised her arm to strike Daniel.

"Please, please watch my arm," said Daniel pitifully.

Rebecca huffed and brought her arm down.

The group began to make their way through the dark gloomy room.

They traveled for more then a half an hour to find an end and a way out.

"AHHHHHHHHHHH!"

Suddenly, Uncle Rain screamed.

Everyone looked to where the scream came from.

"Where is he? Where's my Uncle?!" asked Aliza, as she looked around her frantically.

"He's gone I can't see him anywhere," said Naomi.

"Gabriella, please use your globe to see if we can find him. Hurry!" said Aliza.

Gabriella made silent howl again.

Suddenly, the fire on the candles burst into flames and shot towards them.

They all dodged it except for Rebecca. She was struck with fear.

The fire hit Rebecca her engulfed her in flames.

"AHHHHHHHHHH!"

Rebecca screamed.

"REBBECCA!!!" screamed Daniel.

Suddenly, the flames around her body diminished.

Rebecca opened her eyes scared out of her wits.

Everyone came towards her to see what damage the flames had on her body.

"What? How could this be?" asked Rebecca to herself.

Rebecca's body and clothes were not burned or singed at all.

"It…it worked," said Daniel to himself, while trying to calm his nerves.

"What worked?" asked Rebecca curiously.

"I...I used the power of Aliza's feather to protect you from ever getting hurt, while we were on our mission," said Daniel, as he looked her in the eyes at a distance.

Everyone was very surprised at his answer.

"You did!" asked Rebecca.

Daniel nodded.

Rebecca walked up to him and looked him in the eyes.

"I never knew you cared that much," said Rebecca.

"Yeah, I never really like to..," said Daniel.

Suddenly, Rebecca kissed him before he could finish.

Daniel felt a warm rush through his body; he couldn't believe he was actually being kissed by Rebecca for the first time. He had never gotten kissed by a girl before.

Rebecca's lips left Daniel's.

"Thank you," said Rebecca with soft eyes.

Daniel blushed.

Everyone stood with an awed expression that was slapped on their faces.

"Okay...well...what do we do about Uncle Rain? He's missing," said Naomi.

"Maybe he was kid napped by one of Killaim's Vieniems or Killaim herself," said Shastekae.

"I don't know. He's always been so wise about Vieniems and their attributes," said Aliza.

"What are you saying, Aliza?" asked Tigerisa.

"All I'm saying...well…I don't know," said Aliza as she looked at the floor.

"So why did he disappear?" asked Taomi still tearing from her lost Leo.

"I don't know." said Aliza.

Everyone started to walk down the dark floor and were still trying to find a way out.

"Where could this room possibly end?" asked Rebecca, as she held Daniel's other hand as they walked.

"I hear something, Mommy," said Jonathan, as he tugged on Naomi's dress.

"What do you hear, baby?" asked Naomi, as she bent down to his level.

"I hear...someone crying," said Jonathan.

"Where?" asked Naomi.

"This way! Follow me!" exclaimed Jonathan, as he ran off into the darkness.

"JOHNATHAN WAIT!" shouted Naomi, as she ran after him.

Everyone ran and followed Naomi.

"AHHHHHHHHH! MOMMY!"

Jonathan screamed.

They all heard many dark deep chuckles.

Everyone found a door way and ran through it as fast as they could to get Naomi's son.

Suddenly, everyone came into a large completely lit hallway with the same flooring and twenty-five foot high stone walls.

They found ten different sized Vieniems surrounding Jonathan.

"What are you doing here, pip squeak?" said one of the Vieniems, as he tugged Jonathan's arm violently.

"LET GO OF MY CHILD, YOU IGNORANT BATS!" yelled Naomi.

Naomi stood in front of the group with her eyes pulsing a deep blue.

Naomi brought out her claws ready to shred all the Vieniems to pieces.

"And who might all of you be?" asked the shortest Vieniem.

"LET GO OF HIM!" shouted Naomi at the top of her lungs.

Suddenly, Naomi transformed and pounced into the air with her claws. She clawed all the Vieniems almost to death.

"Naomi enough!" exclaimed Aliza.

Naomi stood stunned by what Aliza just said.

"Mommy, You Saved me!" yelled Jonathan, as he hugged Naomi.

"Why did you say that, Aliza?" asked Tigerisa.

"If we are to bring peace to both of our kinds, it does not begin with a slaughter. It will only make them hate us even more," said Aliza firmly.

"But they were going to hurt, Jonathan," said Naomi.

"They were only following orders. I'm sure Killaim told them to keep us from entering her throne room. She probably didn't want to be disturbed," said Aliza calmly.

"Who cares if she doesn't want to be disturbed I'll bother her anyway. If I had the chance I'd kill her right now," said Shastekae angrily, as he began to march in front of them.

Suddenly, Aliza grabbed hold of Shastekae's shoulder.

"She's your sister...your own flesh and blood. I'm sure she didn't mean to use her poison to turn you evil and I'm sure both of your parents wouldn't want you to hurt or kill each other either." said Aliza with a serious look on her face.

Shastekae turned his head slightly.

"Then what did she use her poisoned blood for?" asked Shastekae angrily.

"She probably wanted to see if you were really her brother. And if she saw your wings she would be sure" said Aliza firmly.

"That's a lame excuse," said Shastekae, as he looked away from Aliza.

"She's probably been very lonely and troubled not having to know the truth of what happened to her family. Haven't you been feeling or wondering the same thing?" asked Aliza.

Shastekae had a tear fall from his eye.

"Yeah, I guess," said Shastekae.

"Then let's go," said Aliza.

Aliza, Shastekae, Naomi, Jonathan, and the rest of the group began to make their way down the hallway to the Killaim's throne and have their next encounter with the Vieniem Leader.

Chapter 39

The Betrayer Hidden Amunst Them

Aliza and the group reached a large wooden door many feet high and twenty feet wide. They could hear someone crying a distance from behind the door.

"Is Killaim behind the door?" asked Taomi, as she shook in fear.

"Yes," said Aliza.

"Let's run! We might escape death if we hurry," said Daniel, as he started to run in the oppisite direction.

Suddenly, Rebbeca grabbed him by the collar of his shirt and choked him back in the group.

Suddenly, Shastekae pounded open the door.

"KILLAIM, I HAVE A HUGE BONE TO PICK WITH YOU!!!" yelled Shastekae.

They found Killaim bursting in tears and around her were broken vases, torn curtains, and broken windows.

Killaim broke and ripped everything in shatters and shreds.

"Why, Killaim? Why would you allow yourself to be so horrible to treat all Lemptions to the extent of killing them?" asked Aliza.

Everyone were shaking and cowering in fear because of Killaim's rage and fiercely pulsing red wings.

Shastekae was beyond the point of anger: he was furious and ready to kill Killaim on the spot.

Killaim's tears flooded the ground beneath her.

"I'm sorry. I'm so sorry," choked Killaim.

"SORRY! SORRY! YOU EVIL FANGED..." yelled Shastekae.

"HA! HA! HA!"

Shastekae was interrupted by a maniacal laugh of a strange in a dark pitch black corner of the room.

"Who are you?" asked Aliza.

"I was behind it all," said the stranger, as he followed with another evil laugh.

"Behind what?" asked Naomi.

"Don't you understand? I killed Aliza's parents and I killed Killaim's and Shastekae's parents. Killaim was being controlled by me as long as I promised that I wouldn't kill all of you," said the stranger with an evil chuckle.

"Killaim is this true?" asked Aliza.

Killaim nodded in bursts of cries.

"Don't you see she is just like her mother, she cares enough to at least give up to after the killing has gone too far. That is why I had to kill her mother before, after she refused to listen to me anymore and follow my orders," said the evil stranger.

"You evil being," said Aliza angrily.

"Your parents on the other hand Aliza. After, I killed your parents I threw you into a wicked family...in hopes you weren't going to be able to find the way to make peace. I hoped I wouldn't have to kill you and those closes to you, so you would give up...such as your husband Zack. You see, Vieniems weren't after you for the stone's power. They were after you because I ordered them to kill you. And the Reinstone Crystal never existed. The Reinstone Crystal was the crystals that your howl grows. The real

Crystal of Light," said the wicked stranger with another evil chuckle.

"YOUR AN EVIL VIENIEM!!!" shouted Naomi.

"I killed the Naomi's and her friend's village and their families. I killed Daniel's parents, and I killed Gabriella's parents, as I left her in the forest of death hoping she'd die or get killed. And I actually injected Vieniem blood in Shastekae's neck when he thought Killaim bit him the time she showed up in the steel area where Shastekae was making Aliza's sword. Killaim didn't bite him at the steel factory. She was just a cover up...and that's how I showed up right away to pretend I was protecting Shastekae from Killaim," chuckled the stranger.

"How could you perform such wicked acts?" asked Aliza.

Everyone around her was burning in anger and ready to kill this murderer.

"I wish to end both your races, but hope to end your spirits first," said the stranger.

"If you're a Vieniem than why would you want to kill your own kind?" asked Aliza.

"Oh...I'm not a Vieniem...in fact...I happen to be human," said the stranger with another evil laugh.

"What is your name?" asked Aliza.

"Vulgare Crane," said the stranger.

Aliza thought that the last name sounded so familiar.

"What's wrong Aliza? Can't you even recognize my voice?......My step niece," said Vulgare.

He laughed loud manically.

Aliza was struck by his last words and a tear fell from her eye.

Suddenly, the stranger stepped out into the light.

It was Uncle Rain!!!

"YOU BACK STABBING SWINE!!!" screamed Naomi.

Suddenly, Aliza's crest glowed a bright blue and her body shot forth gold and blue light above them and bursted through the ceiling and into the cloud filled sky. Then green lighting shot around her destroying the room and left nothing but ruble. The dark clouds above them began to circle.

Everyone trembled at Aliza's immense power, but the lighting never hit them.

Everyone looked over the edge and found they were on the very top of Killaim's castle that stood on the top of the highest Mountain of Chaos.

Suddenly, blue light from the clouds surrounded Vulgare Crane.

Then the blue light suddenly became fire, but just before Vulgare Crane was about to be killed Vulgare pulled out a green stone whistle and blew.

Suddenly, Aliza's crest burned out and she fell to her knees unconscious.

"What did you do to her!?" shouted Naomi and the others.

They all surrounded her for protection.

"I made this whistle from stone that was deep in your planet that would stop even the chosen one's stone from its powers. I was the one who ended up destroying your planet, so your two races would fight to the end of extinction. I worked for a secret organization that travels the solar system in attempt to make sure humans would be the top ranking beings in the universe. I used government technology to create a space ship and find aliens to destroy, so that humans were the only ones to exist in our entire solar system. Killaim's and Shastekae's mother discovered the truth before I killed her, which is the same thing that is going to happen to you now," shouted Vulgare Crane laughing loud with an evil smirk of satisfaction.

Killaim suddenly, joined the group to surround Aliza's body.

"I am so sorry about the things that I did," said Killaim.

"Oh, just forget about it!" shouted Shastekae, still angered.

"HA HA HA HA!" laughed Vulgare Crane.

"NOW!" shouted Vulgare, as his voice echoed in the air.

Suddenly, a hundred Vieniems surrounded them.

"HE'S GOING TO KILL ALL OF YOU TOO!!!" shouted Killaim.

"Not if we obey his orders to the end, unlike you!" said the largest Vieniem.

"KILL THEM ALL!" laughed Vulgare Crane.

"RUN!" screamed Daniel.

"For once you are right," shouted Rebecca in a shaky voice.

They all began to run back down the hall, but they found another hundred Vieniems blocked of their path.

Vulgare than met them with the other Vieniems behind him.

"Ready to die," said Vulgare Crane with an evil grin.

Suddenly, Aliza eyes opened slightly.

"ALIZA, MAKE A VERY STRONG SHIELD QUICK! I'LL STOP THEM!" said Daniel strong.

"With what?" said Rebecca with a quivering voice.

"MY HOWL!" said Daniel, as he looked at Vulgare with an evil grin.

"You wouldn't dare." said Vulgare Crane with a sudden expression of fear.

"YOU BET!" said Daniel.

"NOW! GET THEM NOW!" shouted Vulgare Crane with a quivering scream of fear.

All the Vieniems darted in for the kill, but Aliza shielded them all with the last of her strength, including Killaim, and kept the Vieniems from getting towards them.

Suddenly, Daniel made a deafening howl that seemed to go for miles.

They all heard a sonic boom in the distance and heard wind blow outside through the trees. Then they heard trees being uprooted and slamming into the sides of the castle.

As this all was happening Vulgare just stood with a look of terror on his face.

"BOOOOOOOOOM!!!"

The castle was obliterated including the rest of the forest in a five mile radius around them. Every thing was destroyed, including Vulgare Crane and the other Vieniems.

They all floated back to the ground unharmed and Aliza's shield disappeared, including the rest of her strength.

Aliza returned to her normal self and Aliza again had her white ears and hair.

Aliza layed unconscious in Shastekae's arms and again showed her pregnancy on her stomach.

Everyone gasped and were speechless by what amazing power Daniel's howl had done.

"I...I n...never knew. Daniel, I'm sorry I laughed," said Rebecca, as she put her hand on Daniel's shoulder.

THUD!

Daniel's body flopped to the ground and just laid there motionless.

"DANIEL! DANIEL! WAKE UP! WAKE UP!" cried Rebecca, as she fell to her knees and shook his shoulders.

Daniel wasn't breathing.

"NAOMI! PLEASE! PLEASE DO SOMETHING!" screamed Rebecca.

"Rebecca quick use your feather," said Naomi.

Rebecca ripped out her feather from her pocket and placed on Daniel's chest and closed her eyes.

The feather was absorbed in Daniel's body.

"Please, Daniel. Please wake up," cried Rebecca, as tears fell from her eyes on Daniel's cheeks.

Rebecca held Daniel in her arms for more than five minutes, but Daniel still wasn't breathing.

"Rebecca, He...he's gone," said Naomi, as she tried to pull her away.

"NO! I DON'T BELIEVE IT! HE'LL BE OKAY! PLEASE BE OKAY!" whispered Rebecca in Daniel's ear.

Rebecca still held him in her arms for another five minutes, but Daniel body was still lifeless.

"Daniel I...I'm so sorry. I never showed you or told you I loved you, even though I really did. I...never took in consideration of your feelings...I always thought of my own. Even though your a pain sometimes...I still love you and I always will...I love you, Daniel." cried Rebecca.

"Rebecca, I'm so sorry," said Taomi.

Rebecca starred into Daniel's lifeless face stained by her tears and kissed his lips. Then she hugged him tenderly.

Suddenly, she felt a hand touch hers and started to feel Daniel's breathing.

"I love you too, and I always will," whispered Daniel's voice in her ear.

"You're...YOU'RE ALIVE!" cried Rebecca happily.

Everyone cheered.

"I won't be able to walk for a while though," coughed Daniel.

Rebecca then hauled Daniel in her arms with her temper's beating exercise, now filled with a guiltyconcience from her constant beating.

When they all started to walk back to the school Killaim just stood still.

"Aren't you coming with us, Killaim?" asked Naomi.

"Are you sure? After all I did...they won't understand," said Killaim sadly, as she starred shamefully at the ground.

"Vulgare Crane is the one to blame, not you. After we explain the truth about what happened to our families and our planet...they'll know the truth." said Naomi.

"It's okay...It's not your fault. You're the one who protected us, so we'll protect you." said Taomi.

"Yeah, let's go you moron of a sister." said Shastekae with a difficult smile.

Killaim smiled at the care and consideration these Lemptions had, now she understood her mother's wish for peace. She was never treated with such love.

Everyone headed back to the castle with the most feared Vieniem in their history, as a misunderstood friend.

Aliza finally made peace with the two races and made it possible for a better future.

Chapter 40

The Birth of a New Age

The group had finally reached the gates of the school and Aliza was awake and walking again.

"Wow this school is amazing! Is this where Lemptions learn?" asked Alexander.

"Yeah!" said Aliza.

"Cool!" said Alexander, as he looked awed at the school.

Daniel was still not able to walk and had passed out over and over again, but Shastekae was now carrying him.

"We need to bring Daniel to the nurse as soon as possible," said Rebecca quickly.

Rebecca was scared for Daniel's safety because of his arm and his weakness. She was ashamed at herself because of what she did to Daniel's arm.

"What if they try to kill me?" asked Killaim with a shaky voice.

"Then we'll protect you," said Naomi.

"Mommy, is this the Lemption's home?" asked Jonathan.

"No, no baby, it's a school, but it could be," said Naomi.

"How can you be so nice to me after what happened?" asked Killaim, as she looked at the ground.

"It was not your fault, Killaim. Is was Vulgare Crane's," said Aliza with a look of disgust after she mentioned her so called Uncle's real name.

"Why don't you transform into your human form?" asked Tigerisa.

Killaim transformed, but still had pointed ears because she was a Vieniem and not a Lemption with furry cat-like ears.

Then they began to walk down the stone pathway and passed all the cottages to the castle.

Lemptions outside their cottages noticed that Killaim was in the group and began to cower in fear.

Once they reached the school they walked inside and made their way to the nurse.

Lemptions walking in the hallways ran at the sight of Killaim.

"You see. They're more afraid of you, then you are of them," said Aliza calmly.

Killaim's nerves began settle.

Suddenly, Principle Hartford was running down the hall to meet them.

"Did you do it? Did you destroy her? Is there peace now?" asked Principle Hartford quickly.

Then he noticed Killaim in the group and began to scour at her and tremble in fear at the same time.

"W...why is sh...she h...here?" asked the principle as his voice quivered.

"She's not to blame. It was Vulgare Crane. He destroyed our planet and he made our races fight. Killaim was following his orders, so that we wouldn't be killed," explained Aliza.

Principle Hartford stood there stunned by Aliza's answer.

"How is that possible? And who is Vulgare Crane?" asked Principle Hartford quickly.

"He's...he's Uncle Rain. He's the one who killed my family and everyone else's families here with mine too, including Killaim's and Shastekae's," said Aliza sadly.

Aliza continued explaining the whole story of Vulgare Crane's plot to Principle Hartford in a long discussion.

Principle Hartford understood and lead them to the nurse's office.

Daniel was laid on one of the beds in the large room.

"Oh yeah...Aliza, I have a surprise for you," said Principle Hartford with a smile.

"What?" asked Aliza curiously.

"Zack!" called Principle Hartford to a curtain by one of the hospital beds.

Aliza couldn't believe what she heard.

Suddenly, her husband walked out from behind a hospital curtain and stood before everyone's eyes.

It was Zack.

Aliza stood stunned and began to cry happily.

"How? How is he alive?" asked Aliza.

"The poison somehow was reversed in Zack's blood stream and he awoke found on the ground crawling by a fellow Lemption, but he still needed urgent care. So he's been here all this time. He was fighting to see you, even though he was still desperately ill. He didn't want you to go on your mission alone. He was very worried," said the Principle with a smile.

Suddenly, Aliza ran to Zack and jumped in his arms.

Zack fell over because he was still very weak.

"Your alive. Your alive. I love you. I can't believe your still alive. I missed you so much. You were gone for so long," cried Aliza happily in his arms.

"I love you too. I'm so sorry I made you so sad," said Zack.

Aliza kissed Zack and embraced him ever so tightly.

Everyone stood there amazed that Zack had made it after all.

"Principle Hartford, Daniel needs help. I broke his arm, but for some reason he almost died because of his howl," said Rebecca, as her eyes filled with tears.

"He howled!?" asked Principle Hartford with a look of terror in his face.

Rebecca nodded.

"He destroyed everything, including Vulgare Crane and the evil Vieniems," explained Naomi.

"Oh my. Daniel Crystalyst, why could you put your life in jeopardy again? I warned you what would happened if you used your howl," said Principle Hartford, as he turned to Daniel slowly.

"I had to! Vulgare was going to kill us all!" said Daniel weakly.

"Why would his life be in jeopardy because of his howl?" asked Rebecca curiously.

"Because... every howl he makes...takes fifteen years off of his life and each time he howls...And the next he howls the damage it causes always becomes stronger," said the Principle, as he looked at the ground.

Rebecca was horrified by his answer.

"Daniel, why did you howl? Why would you do such a thing?" asked Rebecca, as she kneeled beside the bed next to Daniel.

Daniel took her hand in his.

"Because I had to save you...losing my life would be worth it, if I saved yours," said Daniel.

Rebecca smiled weakly and kissed him for a long moment.

"Don't do it again or I'll have to break your arm again," said Rebecca with a smile.

Daniel smiled and they kissed again.

Zack and Aliza finally met up with the group.

"Daniel...please don't howl again," said Aliza with a weak smile.

Suddenly, Aliza cried out in pain.

"Aliza, Aliza what's wrong!" yelled Zack.

Aliza fell to her knees.

"Nurse... nurse come quick!" yelled Zack.

Aliza cried out in pain again.

The nurse came and pulled Aliza on a bed.

"They're coming. Aliza's going to give birth any minute," said the nurse as she felt her stomach.

Everyone stood stunned by what the nurse just said.

"Zack, Your going to be a daddy!" exclaimed the nurse.

The nurse suddenly pulled curtains around Aliza, as Zack walked toward Aliza and held her hand.

Everyone waited a distance away from the bed where Aliza was giving birth.

They heard Aliza cries of pain and agony.

Suddenly, everyone heard a baby's cry.

Aliza let out another cry of pain.

They heard another baby's cry.

Then there was silence.

Two minutes later the nurse pulled back the curtains.

"You can come over now," said Zack excitedly.

Everyone walked up to where Aliza was laying and she was holding two babies.

"We have a boy and a girl," cried Aliza happily.

"What are you going to name them?" asked Naomi with happy tears coming out of her eyes.

Aliza looked up at Zack and he nodded.

"We'll name the girl, Lily, and the boy, Zack jr," said Aliza with a smile.

They all cried happily and took turns holding the babies.

The baby girl had bright red hair and red ears and pink eyes with a yellow diamond shaped crest in her forehead.

The baby boy had white hair and white ears with purple eyes and had a dark purple diamond shaped crest on the back of his neck.

"Why do they both have crests?" asked Tigerisa.

"I thought only The Chosen One was suppose to have The Yemuel Crystal Crest, Aliza," said Naomi.

Aliza shrugged her shoulders.

"They're so cute," said Kim.

Alexander gazed at the babies happily.

Jonathan laughed at the funny sounds the babies made.

Shastekae, Killaim, the rest of the group, and Principle Hartford smiled at the happy moment.

Zack felt very proud that he was a father.

When night came about Aliza and Zack slept together happily on the hospital bed while everyone slept in sleeping bags on the floor. The babies were put to sleep in craddles next to Zack and Aliza.

"WAAAAAAAHHHHHHHHHH!"

Aliza's and Zack's baby boy let out a loud cry and they woke up and looked in Zack jr.'s craddle.

Everyone opened their eyes immediately and ran to the baby boy's craddle.

Zack jr. was gone.

Everyone gasped.

They saw that Lily was still sleeping in her craddle.

"Where is Zack jr.!? Where is my baby!" cried Aliza loudly.

Zack was filled with anger.

"What's that?" asked Jonathan.

They all noticed there was a burned sheet of paper in the craddle.

The words were written in blood.

"Dear step niece,
   Thanks for the little prize. He'll grow up in my care now and become my trainee. And don't try to catch me or he'll dye.
Vulgare crane"

"No, it can't be…he…he should be dead!" said Aliza in a shaky voice.

"He couldn't have survived!!!" said Daniel in shock.

"He survived!?" said Naomi.

"We have to catch him," said Zack.

"No! If we chase him! He'll kill our little Zack jr.!" exclaimed Aliza frightened.

"That rotten no good..," said Zack.

Aliza bursted in loud cries and was rivering tears.

Zack held her close, still fuming in anger.

Everyone couldn't believe what had just happened, but were ready to get the child back the first chance they got.

All of these jpgs will go in this order starting on the next page with the title in bold and underlined Algerian font size 36. Each alphabetical letter will go next to each symbol according to the name of each jpg in the bottom right hand corner with the same font, but not underlined or in bold.

THE ANCIENT
LEMPTION LANGUAGE

ANCIENT LEMPTION LANGUAGE A

ANCIENT LEMPTION LANGUAGE B

ANCIENT LEMPTION LANGUAGE C

ANCIENT LEMPTION LANGUAGE D

ANCIENT LEMPTION LANGUAGE E

ANCIENT LEMPTION LANGUAGE F

ANCIENT LEMPTION LANGUAGE G

ANCIENT LEMPTION LANGUAGE H

ANCIENT LEMPTION LANGUAGE I

ANCIENT LEMPTION LANGUAGE J

ANCIENT LEMPTION LANGUAGE K

ANCIENT LEMPTION LANGUAGE L

ANCIENT LEMPTION LANGUAGE M

ANCIENT LEMPTION LANGUAGE N

215

ANCIENT LEMPTION LANGUAGE O

ANCIENT LEMPTION LANGUAGE P

ANCIENT LEMPTION LANGUAGE Q

ANCIENT LEMPTION LANGUAGE R

ANCIENT LEMPTION LANGUAGE S

ANCIENT LEMPTION LANGUAGE T

ANCIENT LEMPTION LANGUAGE U

ANCIENT LEMPTION LANGUAGE V

ANCIENT LEMPTION LANGUAGE W

ANCIENT LEMPTION LANGUAGE X

ANCIENT LEMPTION LANGUAGE Y

ANCIENT LEMPTION LANGUAGE Z